Neon
Afterlife

Robert A. Kramer

Copyright © 2019 Robert A. Kramer

All rights reserved.

ii

DEDICATION

*For my wife, who inspires every love story
I'll ever write.*

ACKNOWLEDGMENTS

Special Thanks to: Heather Boltz, Nicole McInnes, David Hull, Matt Sugerik, Sidney Kramer, Jackson Kramer, Stacy Kramer, and all of my beta readers for their feedback.

CHAPTER ONE:

$\mathcal{A}$lex snatched a pair of ballet slippers from a

hook next to her mirror and shoved them into an

overflowing backpack. Beneath these, on a gently worn

dresser, rested a framed picture of a woman in a tutu

with the words *Miami City Ballet Company* scrawled

across the bottom of the image. Alex paused in her rapid,

angry packing when she caught a glimpse of the photo -

her mother.

She looked at herself in the mirror. Her hair

hung loose around her face, framing sad eyes. She

resembled the woman in the photo, but her hair color

1

was different, a dark brown like her father instead of her mother's sandy blond. She stared hard at herself for a moment and sighed, "Happy birthday, baby."

Another small photograph caught her attention. In it, three people posed on stage smiling together with arms holding one another as family should. Her father, with gentle brown eyes and a soft handsomeness, her mother with a dancer's physique and a proud smile, and Alex, 12 years old, wearing a leotard and holding a bouquet of roses. She took the photo and traced the image of her mother's face gently with her finger before shoving the picture into her backpack too.

Dozens of trophies rested on a shelf, not a speck of dust on them. Framed photographs of Alex in various dance costumes at ages ranging from six to sixteen occupied every open space on the wall surrounding the golden statues. Amongst the trophies sat a small jewelry box which she roughly opened to grab the wad of money inside, shoving it into her pocket. She flung the backpack over her shoulder and looked back at the room with a mix of longing and resentment, then flicked the light switch off and went out.

Alex slowed down as she approached the couch in the living room. The smell of booze and moldy food caused her to wrinkle her nose. She dropped her backpack to the floor, plopped down on the threadbare cushions and stared intently across the room. Empty beer bottles, syringes, a bent spoon, and greasy pizza boxes littered the place. Her father laid slouched in a recliner, unconscious. She looked at him with disgust, "I hate you."

She got up and grabbed his cell off of the table next to his chair, opened the video app and hit record. Her voice shook, raw, "I really hate you and I'm leaving. Don't look for me because I'm not coming back." She swallowed, trying to maintain her poise. "We had it all. We were special. I was special."

Contempt edged into her voice, "I hate what you've become. What you did to me... to us." She turned her gaze to a window, seeking mental escape, "I miss her too, you know. She left me too. But *I* didn't fall apart. Life goes on, but you forgot about life. About me."

She looked back across the room, anger her steadying force, "Well, you won't have to worry about me anymore. Good bye, Dad." She stopped the recording and tossed the phone onto his lap.

No response.

She stared at him for a long moment. She remembered family picnics and laughing together at corny jokes - when he was healthy. When they were all together. She leaned over and kissed him on top of the head as she fought back her tears and whispered, "I hate you." She picked up her backpack and as she opened the front door of the house to leave she stole a last glance at her father, unmoving except for the soft rise and fall of his chest as he breathed. She slipped through the door, latching it gently behind her.

∞∞∞∞

CHAPTER TWO:

Miami, the warm night air carried the scent of

salt from the ocean, across the beach, and into the city. It

drifted between high rise condominiums and office

towers; where the aspiring wealthy spent over eighty

hours each week attached to their computers and mobile

phones, hustling deals. Through barrios the wind blew,

rustling palm fronds and the hair of children playing

baseball in the streets. It mingled with the scent of

Espresso Colada and Café Cubano as it chased the

exhaust from a bus into the city station. The bus that

Alex, carrying only her backpack, stepped out of.

She caught moments of people moving through the station, snatches of conversations, as she tried to get her bearings amidst the chaotic rush and swirl of humanity around her. Families, businessmen, immigrants, and teenagers brought the place to life, an energy that a girl from a small Southern town had never experienced. Her innocence was apparent to anyone who may have been watching. And someone was.

A slick, good-looking man, dark hair combed back, expensive shoes, and a loose blazer suddenly took her arm in a gentle, but unrelenting grip and started to walk with her, "Señorita, it looks like you could use a guide." He had hard eyes, cold.

"No, I'm fine." She said as time seemed to slow down and speed up simultaneously. She knew something was wrong, in her gut and she tried to pull away, but found his fingers, while not uncomfortable, also would not budge. As he continued to guide her towards the exit, her stomach began to twist in knots. Her mind raced. What was happening? Should she scream?

A voice cut through the ambient hum of humanity, "Liz. Lizzie." A guy in his early twenties, lean and with a graceful strength in his stride, approached them - looking straight at her. He wore a beaten leather jacket that carried its age like a badge of honor and jeans that had too many holes to be trendy, and he had his sights fixed on Alex. "Lizzie. Where are you going?" He said, "I'm supposed to pick you up."

The man holding her arm stopped, his hand locked like a vice. Staring at the interloper, he looked at Alex out of the corner of his eye. She knew he was watching her closely. She had to choose; play along with this new stranger or disappear at the hands of slick.

"Who's this?" the new guy, who was calling her Lizzie, asked.

"Get lost," the man gripping Alex's arm replied.

"We don't have time for this now." The new guy grabbed Alex's hand and pulled. She didn't know him, but his hand was soft, warm. There was a confidence in his touch that she felt surge into her, giving her strength.

Her eyes darted back and forth between the two of them, recognizing that she was suddenly the rope in a tug-of-war between strangers; one of whom had clear intentions and they weren't for her benefit. But the new guy didn't let up and she was thankful. She didn't know why he was helping her or why she thought he was any better than the first guy, but she had a feeling; a connection, like she'd known him all her life. As he moved next to Alex and her captor, his body pressed against hers with a reassuring pressure as he forced his way between them.

Slick, surprised by this unexpected interference, let her arm slip free momentarily. That was all the new guy needed and he gave Alex a good pull to get her moving. "Come on."

Alex let him guide her another direction with quick, purposeful strides.

"Wait," Slick said. He clutched at Alex's retreating backpack, barely getting a finger hold. "She's coming with me." He tried to reel in his catch before it

8

was too late.

"Keep going," the new guy commanded. He shot a glare over his shoulder, locking eyes with the other man. "Let go," he demanded.

The man's control slipped. He was sure he could handle this boy, but what he didn't want was attention. And this moment was quickly escalating to be more trouble than it was worth. He knew he could just grab another girl later. One was the same as another to him; just something to be sold. He hesitated.

Alex tugged her bag free and they moved quickly towards a Metro Policeman lounging near the exit. Close enough to the officer to feel safe, they paused and looked back into the crowded station. The new guy turned to her and gave her a silly half grin as he ran his free hand through his hair. He cast his eyes to her hand, "My name's Jason. I won't hurt you." He said, "But he would've." He nodded towards the man that was quickly melting back into the crowd, looking for a new victim.

"Let go." Alex separated her hand from his, even

though part of her wanted to keep them entwined. "I don't know you either."

"I told you, I'm Jason." As if his name said it all. "And you are..."

"Not Liz."

He chuckled, "Yeah, that would've just been weird if I got that right. Look, come outside." He motioned for her to follow him and then exited the station. Alex stood indecisively as the crowd thinned, her mind whirled. This whole episode had happened so fast, but yet it felt like an eternity. Most people had departed for their destinations, but she could still feel eyes on her. It sent shivers down her spine and she quickly decided to move outside after Jason.

He stood looking tranquil, staring out across the streets towards the airport nearby. She quietly approached and stood next to him. He smiled and glanced her way, assessing the tight jeans and small, denim jacket she was wearing. He looked back at the city.

"It can't really be this beautiful, right?" he said, almost to himself. "Gotta be hiding something."

"My mother loved Miami," she said.

He reached out wide, embracing the city and spun around, "Where street lights will reveal your best kept secrets or you can disappear without a trace."

"Why did you help me?"

"Looked like you could use it."

"I can take care of myself," she said, "You were watching me."

He nods, "I watch everybody."

"Lucky me then."

"Lucky you," he smiled at her playfully. "Not Liz."

She laughed lightly as the tension dissipated, "Alex."

He put out his hand. She took it, glad to feel his warm strength again, and looked into his eyes. They were gentle, honest.

"Well, Alex. What brings you to this magical place?"

"Do you always hang out at bus stations?"

He shrugged, "Only when I'm looking for girls to impress. Are you with a company?"

"What?"

"A company. You're a dancer right?"

"How'd you... no, I..." Alex stammered as she tried to understand how this stranger suddenly knew so much about her.

"Your posture. Your fluid movements," he said, sensing her confusion, "And the ballet slippers peeking out of your bag." He pointed over her shoulder into the partially opened backpack.

She slung the bag off of her shoulder and stuffed her shoes further in, making sure it zipped completely. "It's not a secret."

"Not from a big city either," he continued, "You were like a baby gazelle in there. So easily picked off from the herd."

"Did you just call me a baby gazelle?"

He nodded and smiled. "We should go somewhere else," he glanced at the entrance to the bus station and the man still lurking about, "Coffee?"

Alex realized that she hadn't eaten any real food in hours and her stomach quietly gurgled at the suggestion. Taking the bus from Hot Springs to Miami took more out of her than she imagined. And this guy, Jason, was odd, but endearing. She wasn't sure she should trust him, but, "I could use some food."

"There's a diner a few blocks away. I'll show you." He started off without waiting for a response. Alex hesitated until her rumbling belly urged her to follow.

A few french fries rested on an otherwise emptied plate and half a mug of coffee cooled in Jason's hand as Alex finished the last of her food.

"My dad used to choreograph the Miami City Ballet and my Mom was a dancer there."

"Connections are good," Jason said as he sipped his drink. "I have connections."

Alex nodded, "I'm hoping to get an audition."

"I could help you with that."

"Are you my personal fixer now?"

"Some people call it a Life Coach."

Alex couldn't figure him out, "Are you for real?"

He shrugged. "I know people."

"From the bus station?"

He pulled out his phone, "Give me your number and I'll call you tomorrow and let you know."

She laughed, "Smooth."

"Okay, here." He grabbed a napkin and snaked a pen from an inside pocket of his jacket. "You call me if you're interested." He scribbled down a phone number and his name on the paper. "I've gotta run." He plopped some money on the table. "Don't take rides from strangers." He stood up to leave.

"Are you just going to leave me here?" She

asked; torn between wanting to find someplace to sleep and wanting to spend more time in Jason's company.

"Got some things I have to take care of... other than you," he smiled warmly. "Call me tomorrow, not Liz." And he left.

Alex stared at his retreating back, admiring the relaxed power of his gait, he was graceful. Who was this guy? Some comic book super hero who rescued damsels in distress then vanished? She watched him through the window as he was quickly absorbed into the bustle of the city and disappeared. How was it that she had she come to Miami to start a new life and already found herself lost and confused? Did all big cities have studly bus station guardians or was he really just a random guy who helped her with nothing in it for himself? Did she really want to see him again? She looked at the napkin with his number on it and shoved it into her pocket.

Alex stood at the entrance to one of the tallest buildings in the city, the Panorama Tower. Eighty-five stories of glistening glass and metal, like a spear piercing the night sky. She wondered how they did it; everything looked beautiful as it reached towards the highest heights, but made out of something so fragile... so breakable. She decided to get a better view.

Inside, luxury surrounded her; products, people, restaurants, and offices, a city unto itself as she made her way to the elevator. Eighty-five stories, she wondered how far up it would let her go before she needed special access. She pushed buttons starting from the top and working her way down until one lit up - seventy-nine. As she exited on the floor, she traveled to the stairs, continuing on her mission only to find her way blocked by a door with locks and an alarm.

A small bribe, a little flirting with a security guard, and the promise of a date sometime in the future that she had no intention of keeping and she suddenly had access to the roof. Careful not to let the door behind her close entirely, Alex strode over to the edge. On one side she could see the beach and the ocean that stretched off until it blended into the dark horizon. On another side, she was confronted with towers of cold steel and concrete that populated downtown. Beneath her, bathed in glowing lights, Miami nightlife thrived. People entered and exited nightclubs, theaters, and restaurants like moths to a flame.

She looked up to the stars, "Is this what you wanted for me, Mom?" She set her backpack by her feet and leapt onto the ledge, perching precariously over everything - on top of it all. "This? What did you love so much about this place?"

She closed her eyes and let the city speak to her. Its busy noises combined with the ocean's surf and a soft breeze in a rapturous cacophony, an urban symphony. The city's music filled her body, running through her veins and warming her blood against the chill of the air. She flexed her feet, lifting herself to her toes as she danced on the edge of life and death. Like a gymnast on a beam, her steps were confident, balanced - superb. Back and forth, fearlessly she embraced the abyss with each step, each spin, each leap.

Without even a slight sway as the wind wrapped around her, she came to a stop facing the ocean once more. Breathing deeply of the salty air, she gathered herself and hopped down back to the rooftop. She fished the photograph of her mother with the words *Miami City Ballet* scrawled on the bottom, "I wish you were here." She traced her mother's figure in the image as she plopped down, resting her back to the ledge and stared into the buildings around her. Lights in the windows illuminated the night like the stars above.

∞∞∞∞

CHAPTER THREE:

$\mathcal{T}$he morning sun reflected off of the white

curved façade of the Miami City Ballet building. Alex

paused on her way in to admire the artistically sculpted

lines. They reminded her of the graceful movements of

the dancers who got to work here. Mustering her

courage, she pushed through the front door. She passed

a dancer's lounge, auditoriums and rehearsal spaces as

she wandered down a hallway lined with photographs

from past performances.

She paused at one to inspect it closer. Something

about the dancer in the photo was familiar. She struggled

to hold back tears as she recognized her mother. She had never seen this picture and it took her by surprise to see it here, though she knew it shouldn't. Her mother had been very talented and well loved, she knew, but here was proof; hanging in a hall of fame of sorts. She gathered her emotions and began to move on until a group of young dancers in leotards and tutus burst out of a studio ahead of her. They rushed past her, entered another door and were gone. The soft sound of their slippered feet padding on the floor receded as the door closed behind them.

Alex remembered the thrill of being a little girl at a dance studio, the pure joy that came from being able to express herself through movement. It felt so right, natural. Until everything turned upside down. She collected her thoughts as she came across the door marked as: Artistic Director, Lidia Rodriguez.

She sucked up her courage and knocked.

"Come in." A woman's voice called from inside and Alex entered.

The office was lined with framed promotional materials from a variety of shows. Reminiscent of the hallway, the decoration emphasized the illustrious history of the company and featured years of productions. Alex was hesitant to look at the images too closely for fear of seeing her mother again and getting emotional. An attractive woman, Lidia, with distinctive red framed glasses sat behind a desk littered with figurines of cats: large cats, small cats, art deco cats, cats stretching, cats playing, cats, cats, cats. A pair of empty chairs and a small couch lent a softer touch to the office.

She looked up expectantly as Alex entered the room.

"Mrs. Rodriguez?" Alex asked nervously.

Lidia raised an eyebrow in acknowledgement and Alex forged on, "I'm Alex. Alex Moorefield."

A shock of recognition played across Lidia's face as she saw her old friend Chantelle Moorefield reflected in this girl's youthful face. She didn't try to hide her surprise and it was immediately followed with a warm smile, "I haven't seen you since you were around one year old. You were just learning to stand at that point. Looks like you mastered it."

She got up and came around the desk, wrapping Alex in a giant hug. Alex weakly responded, unsure of what to do. It seemed like an invasion of her personal space, but she wasn't sure she minded.

"I'm so sorry about your mother," she said as she released Alex to get a better look at her. "Chantelle and I danced together before you were born you know. How's your father? Is he with you?"

"Mom mentioned you a few times. That's one reason I stopped by."

Lidia nodded, "How old are you now?"

"Eighteen."

"You dance?"

Alex nodded, "I was hoping I might audition for the school. The pre-professional program? See if I could get a scholarship?"

Lidia leaned against her desk and motioned for Alex to sit. She settled into an empty chair while Lidia looked her over more carefully; the wrinkled clothing, the backpack, the dirt that would normally be washed off of a teenage girl... "We aren't having any auditions until spring. Are you able to wait that long?"

Alex stared at her feet, "I'm kinda on my own here."

"Your father?"

Alex shook her head, "Doesn't know where I am and I don't want him to." A small fire simmered behind her eyes emphasizing the pointed response.

Lidia caught on quickly and raised her hands in surrender, "Got it. Listen, even if I could get you an audition. Even if you got in. You'd have to pay for it if you didn't get a scholarship."

"I want to be a professional dancer. Like my mother. I'll do whatever it takes. If you get me an audition, I can handle the rest."

"Where are you staying?"

Alex shrugged, "I've got a room for now at one of those long stay motels. I was hoping to stay in student housing." She looked at her feet.

Lidia looked concerned and asked, "You have some money?"

"A little," Alex answered, "left from my mom's life insurance."

Lidia flinched, "Enough to get you through to spring?"

Alex shrugged again. "I hadn't thought about needing it that long. I guess I might need to reconsider some things if that's my only option."

"Why don't you come to dinner at my place tonight? We could talk more. Here's my address." She scribbled on a yellow sticky note and passed it to her, "Six?"

"Okay, thanks." Alex got up to leave. She felt dejected and her body language showed it.

Lidia's heart hurt for this young girl. She had no mother and her father was clearly not an option, maternal instincts took over. She could tell Alex needed something, anything to hold on to at that moment, "Do you want to see the school before you go?"

Alex perked up at the opportunity, "I'd like that."

∞∞∞∞

CHAPTER FOUR:

$\mathcal{A}$ taxi pulled up to the curb in front of a small,

well landscaped home. A lone palm tree occupied the

front yard, reminding Alex of a postcard image of Florida

as she climbed out of the back seat and slung her

backpack over her shoulder.

The cab drove off leaving Alex indecisive on the

sidewalk until Lidia opened the front door with a

welcoming smile. Alex smiled back and made her way to

the entrance.

"I'm sorry," said Lidia, "I didn't realize you

didn't have a car. I would have given you a ride from the school."

"That's okay," Alex shrugged, "I need to learn my way around."

Lidia moved aside so Alex could enter. She gently set her bag just inside the door as she took off her shoes. The house was simple and warm, not overly ornate or pretentious; cozy. It reminded her of her home, before the accident.

She looked around, searching.

"The bathroom is in the hall if you need to use it."

"Oh, uh... no, thanks." Alex blushed. "I like cats and I was just looking for yours."

"We don't have one." Lidia smiled.

"But you have all of those cat figurines in your office?"

"I'm allergic." She ushered Alex into the kitchen. "Sometimes you can admire and love something that you can't have. I love cats. So sleek and graceful. I just can't own one. You work with what you have." She shrugged and smiled at Alex.

In the kitchen, a well-built man in his late 40s, with a shock of black hair, worked at the stove top. His apron proudly proclaimed him "chef". The smell of roasting plantains permeated the air.

"This is my husband, José." Lidia motioned for Alex to sit at the table as she introduced her to her husband. "This is Alex."

He wiped his hands on his apron and walked over to shake Alex's hand. "I hope you like Cuban food."

"I don't think I've ever had Cuban food before."

"Then your life has yet to begin," he smiled at her.

Lidia smiled too, "He's an excellent cook."

"It's one of my two passions," he said.

"What's the other one?" asked Alex.

"My wife," he winked at Alex and smiled

mischievously towards his wife.

Alex felt awkward, she couldn't remember the last time her parents were together like this. Her memories were all of her father's downward spiral after her mother died. Fast food and garbage. Not cooking and enjoying each other's company. She thought about finding an excuse to bail out, but the joy of the moment drew her in. Is this what family was supposed to be like? What she missed out on? Why couldn't she have had this? Maybe she didn't get it with her family, but she decided she might get it now, "Can I help?"

José looked at her surprised, "You want to cook?"

She nodded.

"Get this girl an apron."

Lidia opened a drawer and grabbed two aprons. She handed one to Alex. They pitched in and helped prepare the food. José slid some vegetables Alex's way and handed her a knife. She immediately got to work chopping while Lidia tossed some spices into a pan. Alex got lost in the moment. There was playful banter between Lidia and José while they cooked. They displayed affection like she remembered her parents having when she was little. It wasn't always awful. They used to have fun together. Her mother's laugh would ring throughout the house and her eyes would sparkle with such joy. And her father... he used to chase her around and play fight with her. He was gentle and kind, like José. She missed them both terribly. It was like they all died in that accident. She shook herself loose from the memories in time to add the vegetables to a pan.

The three of them sat at a table full of empty dishes; very little remained of the evening meal. Their aprons were haphazardly strewn about the kitchen and Alex soaked in as much of the moment as she could, letting it build in her memory so she could hold onto it. Just for a little longer.

"Listen, I have some tough news." Lidia got serious for a moment. "I talked to the director of the school. He won't make any exceptions for auditions. I'm sorry. I really tried."

Alex sunk into herself as tears sought to break free. She's didn't cry, not anymore. She had stopped doing that, but right now she wasn't sure she could hold it together. She just wanted to have something to keep her going. Her world had been so bleak, but this time with Lidia and José showed her what life could be. She had bet everything on getting in to the dance school. It was her ticket to this kind of life. It was her destiny. She knew it in her soul. But apparently no one else did.

José put his arm across her shoulders, "It'll be okay."

She wanted to shrug him off, but she wanted him to embrace her in a fatherly hug too. Just to remember what that was like. "This was all I had. It was everything."

"It's not that long of a wait." He tried to comfort her with a gentle squeeze. "You can come back and audition with everyone else. I'm sure you'll make it in."

He shared a helpless look with his wife.

Alex scrubbed at her eyes with the back of her hand. "I promised her," she said. "She was laying there looking at me, holding my hand. I promised her I'd be just like she was."

"You still can," said Lidia. "Just not--"

The front door slammed. "What's for dinner?" A young man interrupted as he walked into the kitchen. He stopped cold in his tracks as he looked at his parents, their expressions, then at Alex. He carefully controlled his surprise at finding her there. She looked back, shocked at his sudden appearance. She was momentarily frozen.

José stood up and put his hands on Jason's shoulders. "This is our son, Jason." He looked at Alex, "This is Alex."

Lidia chimed in, "Jason is a student at the school. Maybe he can give you some insider information."

"We've actually met." Alex responded.

Jason joined in almost too quickly, "I saw her at the school today, actually."

Alex was confused, but knew when to stop talking. There was more going on here than she was aware of and she was going to wait and find out before she spoke again.

"I don't remember introducing you?" Lidia said.

"It must've been when you weren't around," he lied.

"You missed dinner."

"I had things to take care of."

José put a hand on his wife's shoulder and she stopped interrogating her son. Silence encompassed them and tension filled the room.

"Thank you for a lovely evening," Alex said as she stood to leave. "I should head out."

"Let me drive you." Lidia offered.

"That's okay. I think I'd like to walk around a little bit."

"You sure?"

"I like to wander."

As they got to the door Jason grabbed her bag. "I'll drive you. It's dark. Miami's not safe at night by yourself."

"Really, I'll be okay."

"Aren't you going to eat?" Lidia asked.

He glanced at his parents and the remaining dregs of food, "I'll grab something when I'm out."

Lidia frowned and folded her arms.

Jason looked back at Alex. "Let me show you around," he pleaded with his eyes. "I'll give you the grand tour." Alex could feel Lidia and José watching them.

She spoke through clenched teeth and a fake smile, "Sure. That would be fun."

She headed out with Jason right behind her.

Alex and Jason rode in his old, red Volkswagen

Beetle in silence. It had flared out fenders, a large subwoofer in back, and a small hole in the floor that Alex could see the street through. The sound of the road droned on as the only noise and street lights flashed by hypnotically until Alex couldn't take it anymore, "What was that about? Why did you act like you met me at the school not the bus station? Why'd you suck me into your escape plan? Is this really your car or is it your Mom's from when she was a teenager?"

Jason wilted under the barrage until the end when he chuckled, "It's my car." He gave her a sheepish grin.

"Watch the road." She crossed her arms and wouldn't look his way. "You can let me out now."

"Nope."

"You're kidnapping me? Is that what you're hiding from your parents? You're a kidnapper."

"I'm not hiding anything from my parents."

Alex rolled her eyes, "I'm not stupid."

He glanced at her out of the corner of his eyes,

while still watching the road.

"I knew that guy at the train station was bad news before you showed up. I was just figuring out what to do when you went all chivalrous on me."

He grinned, "You thought I was chivalrous?"

"Until you abandoned me at the diner." She folded her arms and glared at him.

"What was I supposed to do?" he asked. "Stay with you all night?"

"Maybe."

"Then you'd think I was after something," he said. "I just wanted to help a pretty girl out."

Alex blushed, "You're changing the subject."

Jason opened his mouth to protest, but no sound could come out before Alex continued, "You're hiding something from your parents. And they're nice. And you shouldn't hide anything from them because you're lucky to have them. And you don't know what you've got. You should be grateful you get a family that loves you, you get to dance, you have a future-"

"My parents want me to be a professional ballet dancer," he blurted out. "I've danced since I could stand up."

"Me too."

"But you like it."

"How do you know that?" she asked.

"The magic of Miami revealed it to me," he chuckled. "You came to get into the school on your own. No one is forcing you."

"And you're being forced?"

He nodded.

"How old are you?" she mocked.

"I like dancing. Just not ballet. It's not what I want to do with my life," explained Jason.

"So, do something else."

"I am. But I have to keep up the ballet for them. They've invested too much."

"You're afraid to tell your parents that you don't

like ballet? Seriously, that's your problem?" she scorned.
"You're a moron."

"Like you've got it all figured out. Living out of a
backpack."

"You don't know anything about me."

He smiled at her mischievously as he pulled the
car into any alley and parked. "I bet I do."

Alex hadn't realized how much ground they had
travelled. They were back in the city. She vaguely
recognized the area, but couldn't quite place it. She
should have been watching where they were going, but
instead she'd let her emotions get the better of her. She
spent the entire drive berating a virtual stranger. What
was wrong with her? She should have been asking
herself all sorts of questions, but instead she asked
Jason, "What are you doing?"

He climbed out of the car, "Come on." He looked
around, pulled his hood up over his head and walked off.
Alex scrambled out of the car and followed him. As they
exited the alley, she spotted the bus station a little ways

off.

"You're taking me to the bus station?" she asked. "I'm not going back."

He kept walking and she jogged to catch up.

"Do you always just walk off and expect girls to follow you?"

"You ask too many questions," he replied. "And you don't need me to tell you what to do. You come if you want to."

"What are we doing?"

He just smiled at her and kept walking. They turned down into a different alley and approached a rusty metal door. He tugged it open and hot air mixed with the smell of sweat erupted from inside, along with a hot Latin rhythm.

He gestured for her to enter as he held the door. She hesitated, but didn't want Jason to think she was afraid. Her curiosity and pride won and she entered, feigning confidence - nose held high as she crossed the threshold. Jason chuckled and shook his head as she passed him.

Music thrummed through the space, encompassing her. Reverberations rattled her bones. As her eyes adjusted to the dim lighting, she could make out dancers whirling on a concrete floor. Their feet dragged and spun, kicking up dust that mixed with the light beams. Perspiration glistened on their bodies as the sight of their sensual movements enhanced the beat that penetrated her to her core.

Jason grabbed Alex's hand and pulled her into the club, deeper. Small, uninhabited tables rested near a rough bar built with concrete blocks and what looked like an old door. The bartender caught Jason's eye and they nodded at each other in greeting.

Each echo of the bass knocked Alex's breath away, "What is this place?"

"The Pendulum."

"What?" she yelled into his ear, over the music.

"It's a club, kind of," he shouted back. "Home."

He led her to a table and sat her down. Leaning

in close, he spoke into her ear, "Watch." His warm breath on her neck sent electric tingles throughout her body. She quickly turned away to look at the dance floor. Her heart synchronized to the rhythm and she let the music fill her... and she watched.

She drank in the passion of the dance, anonymous limbs whipped and whirled, hair and hands blazed under the strobes. Hips gyrated as they pushed the limits of Latin tradition, combining it with street style freezes and break dance pops and locks. The fluidity of the movement mesmerized her. Intoxicated, she leaned towards the floor watching bodies and skin, everything pulled her towards the bacchanalian reverie.

Jason seized the opportunity and grabbed her out of her seat, spinning her onto the dance floor. Organically, space opened up for them as dancers parted allowing the new pair into the mix of bodies, swirling and pulsating with the beat. Alex hesitated, but Jason took a firm hold of her hips and started to move her to the music.

"What are you doing?" she asked.

He smiled, "Dancing." He stepped towards her so close that their bodies pressed together. She stepped back, away. Again he pressed against her. She pushed back into him this time. He shifted directions and she followed. Soon they moved as one. Bodies pressed against each other, sweating, glistening in the vortex of dust and light. Transfixed by the rhythms and each other.

They inhaled acoustic ecstasy with each breath and let it fuel their muscles until all sense of time was lost; absorbed in the moment, this moment. Their hands found each other's backs or thighs or necks, sharing their heat, tracing lightning and searing their senses. Their breathing edged against an intimate passion. Enraptured, they became one, lost together as the world vanished around them.

∞∞∞∞∞∞

CHAPTER FIVE:

*E*xhilaration mixed with exhaustion as the

night's music drifted to an end and the lights came up. The other dancers moved off of the floor and began to exit the club.

"Hungry?" asked Jason.

Alex nodded, "How long were we dancing?"

"Hours."

They found their way back to the diner that Jason brought her to the previous night. Between them rested a plate full of french-fries. Nearly empty glasses of ice cold water sat in their hands, the condensation cooling their palms. Adrenaline still pumped through their veins as they enjoyed the quiet hours before the dawn.

"What do you think?" asked Jason.

"About what?"

"The Pendulum."

Alex looked deep into his eyes, "It's amazing."

"Do you ever feel like that when you're doing ballet?" he asked. "I don't."

Alex shook her head, "Different. That was aggressive. Primal. For me, ballet embodies eloquence, refinement... control."

He nodded, "I'm tired of control."

"What were you doing at the bus station last night?"

"Can we talk about something else?"

"I barely know you," she said. "I want to know more."

Jason flushed in embarrassment a little and he

sighed, "I go there to think."

"There?"

"I can be alone there."

She looked at him quizzically.

He continued, "I'm surrounded by people, but they don't know me, notice me, or care if I even exist. And I can watch."

"You go... to be alone?"

"And watch," he said. "All sections of humanity come through there on any given night. The forgotten and the refined. It gives me insight into the world."

"That's deep," she mocked playfully.

"I'm serious. I've been so locked up with what my parents want me to do that I never get to experience the rest of the world."

"It's not so great."

"I wouldn't know," he answered.

"Then how'd you find The Pendulum." Alex asked.

"I followed somebody one night."

"You're a creeper," she laughed. "Was it a girl?'

Jason laughed and nodded.

"Isn't the bus station an odd place to pick up girls?'

"I met you there."

She glared at him. "I threw your number out as soon as you walked away."

"No you didn't"

"I did," she protested. "I thought you were crazy. That I was lucky to survive last night."

He leaned across the table and whispered, "What do you think now?"

"Now, I know it." She pushed his face back until he was sitting back in his seat and they laughed some more. Jason looked out the window.

"You ever see the sunrise over the ocean?" he asked.

She shook her head.

He pulled some money out of his pocket, slapped it on the table and tugged her out of her seat.

"Hey," she exclaimed as he dragged her out of the diner.

The sun peeked above the horizon as Jason and Alex strolled along a path on Miami Beach. The breaking waves called to them as they paused under a canopy of palm trees and looked out at the water. His fingers brushed hers as they stood side by side. She wanted him to put his arm around her. To be absorbed in the romance of this moment, but he held back.

"My mother loved the beach," Alex said. "And the ocean."

"Do you?" Asked Jason.

"I remember holding her hand as we walked on the sand. The warm sun above. It was paradise." She sensed the faint brush of his hand against hers. A gentle intimacy.

"I like the shades of pink and orange as the light

reflects off of clouds," he said. "The smell of salt in the air. The keening of the gulls."

"Keening? Seriously?" she said as he turned to face her, fully taking her hand in his and captivating her with his gaze.

"Before, the sun left my flesh wanting," Jason searched her eyes.

"Tomorrow, I'll feel its obsession.

Before, the wind howled its defiance.

Today, it fills my wings and I soar.

Before, the moon hid from my glancing.

Tonight, I reveled in its passing.

Before, words had no meaning.

To me now, whisper secret tidings.

Before, love looked upon me forsaken.

Together, I am restored."

Alex stared at him in silence for a moment as the morning breeze swirled around them. "What was that?" she asked.

"Poetry."

"But... why?"

"It's what I do."

Alex waited patiently for him to go on. After a moment he sighed in resignation and explained, "Remember when I said Ballet isn't what I do?"

She nodded.

"I write poetry... in the bus station." Embarrassment once again caused his cheeks to flush.

Alex giggled, "You wrote a love poem in the bus station?"

He shrugged. "Some of it. I finished it just now."

"Just now?"

He nodded and it was her turn to blush, "I like it," she said. "What do you call it?"

"Alex."

She punched him in the arm. "Don't be a jerk."

"What did I do?" he asked in astonishment.

"Don't play me."

"I'm not."

She stomped off a few paces and spun to face him. Her anger rising as the feeling of connection was severed so abruptly by Jason's forwardness. It felt... phony. "You kidnap me from your parent's house in your sensitive-man-car, take me dancing all night, and then bring me to watch the sunrise on the beach. You recite a poem you just finished, about me. I'm not an idiot. That stuff only happens in movies or when someone's getting played and this isn't Hollywood."

"I'm not playing you," he protested. He was beginning to look like a puppy that was being scolded and that made Alex even madder.

"You're this gorgeous, ballet-dancer-poet who knows the bartender at the sexy underground club where you take this girl you just rescued from a slimeball at the bus station." She stunned herself with this revelation as she paced back and forth. "This can't be real. You can't be real. Are you secretly a prince too? Or maybe just a wealthy CEO of a big corporation?"

"Did you say gorgeous?" he smirked.

His charm was so disarming, but she couldn't let him in. She had too much to lose, too much to do. She couldn't let a boy get in the way of her promise to her mother. She mashed her palms into her eyes then looked at him to confirm he wasn't a mirage. He was still there. "Either you're a bad cliché or too good to be true. Neither one is what I need right now." She backed off further, "I've gotta go."

He stepped towards her and she retreated more. "Don't," she said as turmoil swirled in her mind.

"Clichés aren't all bad," he pleaded.

She shook her head, confused. "This can't be happening. It's like some Nicholas Sparks parallel universe." She looked at Jason as he stood helplessly watching her. She wanted him to grab her and hold her, but that's not what was happening. He was just... staring.

She turned and jogged off half wanting him to catch her. She needed time to think, alone. But she really liked him and wanted to lose herself in him, too.

"Wait," he called after her. Too late. He watched her retreating figure, wondering if he should have gone after her, until she was gone; obscured by the city and the distance between them.

He wandered back to his car and climbed in; dazed. At the foot of the passenger seat he noticed Alex's backpack. He smiled and turned the ignition.

∞∞∞∞

CHAPTER SIX:

Lidia stared intently at the glowing laptop on

her desk at the Miami City Ballet. A long string of

unanswered emails filled the screen. She sighed as she

scrolled through them before selecting one to read. A soft

rap at her door interrupted her before she was able to get

engrossed in her work.

"Come in."

Alex entered Lidia's office, wearing the same

clothes that she had been wearing the day before. Bags

under her eyes indicated that she hadn't slept much.

Lidia smiled at her, but a kind of motherly concern

mixed with her enjoyment of Alex's visit.

"It's good to see you," Lidia said as she motioned to a chair. "I wanted to talk to you about last night."

"Is Jason here?" asked Alex abruptly.

"I wanted to apologize for how things went after dinner."

"I think I left my bag in Jason's car. I really need to find him."

Lidia's demeanor shifted as she examined Alex's appearance more closely. Her clothes and hair were disheveled and she looked exhausted.

"Are you okay?" she asked. "Jason dropped you off alright?"

"We went dancing and then to the beach. That bag is all I have right now." Alex was near to her breaking point and Lidia could tell.

"Can you please just tell me where he is?" Alex asked.

Lidia stood and moved towards Alex, protectiveness flared up in her for this girl whom she barely knew, but was here anyway, in her office. This girl who had nothing and was so distraught. This girl who reminded her so much of herself and her friend Chantelle when they were young dancers trying to make their way in the world. But they had support, Alex was alone.

"He should be in class. Second floor, room 207," she answered. "If he bothered to show up."

"Thanks."

Alex nearly leapt out of her chair, but before she could get to the door Lidia had a hand gently placed on her shoulder. Alex stopped and Lidia slowly turned her around face-to-face, then wrapped her arms around her in a hug. Speechless, Alex didn't struggle to get away, but she didn't respond either.

"Whatever it is you're going through," Lidia said, "you'll get through it." Alex hadn't been held by a women in that way in years and she was unprepared for the flood of emotions it elicited within her. What was she supposed to do? This was all so... Lidia rubbed Alex's back, "Everything will be alright."

Confused, Alex felt smothered by the embrace and at the same time comforted. Finally, Lidia let go and looked her in the eye, "Room 207."

Alex watched through a window in the door to room 207. A group of dancers practiced a routine. It didn't take long for her to spot Jason.

She watched as he leapt, as he lifted a ballerina and carried her across the floor, and as he strode purposefully and gracefully. She couldn't help but imagine herself dancing with him. His hands around her waist. She felt the searing heat of his touch from the night before when they connected so deeply on the dance floor at The Pendulum.

She watched as the ballerina he practiced with watched him too, enthralled; devouring him with her eyes.

His techniques were impeccable, but there was no passion in his movement. Nothing primal like last night. His dance felt empty. She was overwhelmed with sadness as she watched the dancers practice until Jason spotted her through the door. Their eyes met and he immediately stopped, excused himself and ran over. The ballerina stared as he exited the room and her glare bored into Alex. But Jason was oblivious, a smile crept across his face as he entered the hallway and shut the door behind him.

"I knew you couldn't stay away," he said.

Playfully disgusted, Alex turned her back to him. "She's into you." She nodded towards the ballerina in the classroom.

"Who?"

"The girl you're dancing with."

Jason looked through the window in the door. "Joy?"

"Joy? Really?" Alex rolled her eyes.

He shrugged. "We've been dancing together for years. She's like a sister."

Alex scrunched up her face, "Not to her."

He shrugged nonchalantly.

"You stole my bag."

"Stole?" He feigned shock and offense.

Alex looked him up and down in his leotard and couldn't help but grin.

"It doesn't look like you have it on you," she confessed.

He smiled, "There's not much I can hide in this." He looked into his classroom at the fellow students waiting for him. "Meet me at the Pendulum tonight," he said. "I really want to talk to you."

"Why can't we talk now?"

"I have to finish class."

"I can wait."

"I don't have it here," he said. "Meet me tonight. I have an idea."

"My whole life is in that bag."

"It's safe. Trust me," he gave her a dazzling

smile. "I have to get back to class."

"Fine," she groaned and he headed back into the room, but not before looking back over his shoulder and giving her a Cheshire grin. Why did he make her feel like she was still in high school?

Alex watched as the dancers took up positions and started again. She longed to be on that floor. To be one of them. It always brought her a sense of security. She belonged there and she knew it. What she wouldn't have given for some security right then. Like a place to sleep for a few hours. That needed to be her priority for the moment. A place to stay. She watched a few more seconds then wandered off.

On her way out, she passed a door labelled *School Director*. She slowed to a stop in front of it, indecision nibbled at her nerves. Maybe she could convince the director. Maybe Lidia wasn't really convincing or secretly didn't want her there. Maybe he just needed to meet her... Maybe this wasn't the best idea. Sleep deprivation doesn't help when trying to make risky decisions, she knew, but decided she had nothing to lose. So, she gathered herself and knocked.

A male voice answered from the other side of the door, "Come in."

She pushed it open and entered to find a man in his mid-fifties, typing on his computer and wearing the most boring glasses she's ever seen; plain black frames. The kind you find at a corner store for reading. They seemed to at least match his plain black jacket over his ordinary white shirt, but they were clean and crisp. His appearance was no nonsense. That's what she got out of that initial impression. And she decided that the direct approach would be the best approach, maybe.

He took off the glasses as she entered and looked at her. She felt suddenly vulnerable and aware of her appearance in a way she hadn't been until he turned his eyes to her, assessing. What was his first impression of her? She was a mess. Could that work in her favor? This was a mistake, but she was in it now.

"Hello?" he greeted her.

Alex's anxieties got the better of her and she stood silently before him.

"What can I do for you, young lady?"

"I'm Alex," she stammered. "Alex Moorefield."

He nodded his understanding. "Hello, Alex. What can I do for you?"

"My mother was a dancer here almost twenty years ago. My father was a choreographer." She paused, looking for some sort of response or recognition. Anything. But his expression was blank as he waited for her to continue. "My mother died a few years ago and since then my father has fallen apart. But she, my mom, always wanted me to become a professional dancer. I always wanted to be a professional dancer."

He ran his hand through his thinning hair. "Please, take a seat." He motioned to a couch on the side of the room.

She shook her head. "I came here because she loved this place, this company, more than anything else."

"I assume you dance well?" he asked.

She nodded.

"Auditions will be held in a little over six months."

"I know," she answered. "I just turned 18 and I'm using every penny to get here and make it in. I was hoping you might make an exception and let me audition now... because of my circumstances."

He sighed, "There are a lot of gifted dancers in Miami. A lot of children of gifted dancers too. If we began making exceptions then we would never cease making them." He folded his hands on his desk and looked at her with compassion. She couldn't maintain eye contact and looked at her feet instead.

"Please?"

"I'm sorry Alex. I knew your parents and I liked them very much, but I have to maintain our policies. That is my purpose as the director of the school. Enforcing the policies is what they pay me to do."

"You knew my parents?"

"I was sad to see them leave the company," he

said. "Your father and I were friends. He was a good man, very much in love with your mother. He practically worshipped her. I can understand why he fell apart without her. He must be in tremendous pain."

"Especially since he's the reason she's dead," Alex mumbled.

"I'm sorry?"

"Nothing," Alex visibly slumped. "Isn't there any way? Anything else?" she begged. "I don't have anywhere else to go."

He leaned back in his chair. "I'm sure you could find a job here in Miami and then try out with the other hopefuls. I have no doubt you'll be successful."

Alex struggled to maintain her composure. "If you'd just watch me."

He shook his head. "It's not that simple. There's an audition committee that sits in and compares all of the candidates and chooses the ones that will be the best fit here. Then there are interviews as well. But the most important thing is that they get to see you dance. The whole committee has to see you dance and agree. It's not up to me. If you apply, I'll make sure that you get an audition this coming season. It's all I can do," he said as he put his glasses back on, "Don't give up." He looked back at his computer screen.

Dismissed, she climbed to her feet, numb. "Thank you," she mumbled and started to leave the director's office.

"Some of our dancers post for roommates on a message board in the student lounge. You should check there."

She gently closed the door behind her.

∞∞∞∞

CHAPTER SEVEN:

After class, Jason gathered his things as Joy approached.

"Who was that?" she asked.

"What?" he replied, caught off guard.

"The girl," said Joy. "Who was she?"

"Joy, we tried dating. Remember, it didn't work," he said. "It was more like we were siblings than romantic interest."

Joy folded her arms and glared at him, "She looked like you found her in a homeless shelter."

He chuckled, "Something like that."

She snorted, her derision obvious.

"Look," said Jason, "not everyone has a trust fund to fall back on. She's a dancer and she wants to be a student here, then join the company. I'm helping her out."

Joy wasn't satisfied, "You're helping her like you help all the girls?"

He shook his head, "It's not like that."

"It's never like that... until it is, right?"

"First you were slamming her. Now you're defending her?" He was baffled at the quick turn of events, "What did I ever do to you?"

Her jaw dropped open and she spun on her heels to storm off, leaving Jason to watch her go. She turned off the lights on him as she left, casting him into darkness. He shook his head as he grabbed his hoodie and put it on.

"Jeez," he mumbled to himself. "There must be some girl code or something I don't know about." He threw his bag over his shoulder and made his way out of the classroom.

∞∞∞∞

CHAPTER EIGHT:

Lidia and José sat across from each other at

their kitchen table. The last vestiges of the evening meal

littered their plates. Jose looked at his wife, she had been

virtually silent the whole meal and, like any married

man, he knew that meant something was wrong. And,

being a good husband, he knew what he had to do.

"What's wrong?"

Lidia was taken aback by his question. She

seemed to snap out of a trance. "What makes you think

something's wrong?"

He smiled at her and didn't answer.

She sighed, "Alex came to see me again today."

"That girl's had a hard way."

Lidia nodded. "She'd been out all night dancing."

"She's young. That's what kids do."

"With Jason."

"How do you know that?"

"She was looking for him."

José nodded.

"I just don't want to see her get hurt more," Lidia said. "She's had enough… inconsistency."

"Jason's a good boy," said José. "He's got a good heart. True heart."

"But you know what he's been like. Never committing to anything. Never seeing anything through."

"Maybe he hasn't found anything he wants to hold on to yet."

"Remember that episode with Joy?"

"She didn't give him any space to breathe. He needs to be himself before he can make any long term decisions like a relationship like that."

"That's what I mean," said Lidia. "He doesn't know who he is, so he uses people to find out who he's not."

"That's deep."

"I'm serious. That's what he's doing at the school. He doesn't even care to graduate. All he has left is to do a showcase, but he's not interested anymore. It's like all that time he invested and it doesn't matter. He's moved on. I don't want to see Alex get used like that."

"What is it about this girl and you?"

"I don't know. She's the daughter of one of my best friends," she said. "She's so much like her I almost forget she's not Chantelle."

"Maybe you need to be careful that you don't force her to be someone she's not."

Lidia nodded, "Maybe."

"And remember who your son is," José finished as he picked up their plates and brought them to the sink.

∞∞∞∞

CHAPTER NINE:

*I*nside the Pendulum, Alex watched as dancers

swayed to the hot Latin rhythms. Sitting at a small table

near the bar, she wondered what she was doing there.

None of this was what she expected. She really thought

she was going to just walk in and get a spot in the

academy? So, stupid. The music washed over her, but

she took no joy in its company. Emotions roiled inside

her. Fear. Desperation. Failure. She should have stayed

in Hot Springs. Everything here was so different.

Including the boys, she thought as she spotted Jason

strolling in.

She watched him as he looked around, scanning. He really was too good to be true. Single, funny, handsome, and he seemed to care about her. After one day? One really great day, given. But, one day? It was all so surreal. It couldn't be genuine. He was using her, he had to be. He spotted her and made his way to the table. Pulling up a chair opposite Alex, he plopped down and smiled. She looked him up and down in return. No bag.

"Been here long?" he asked.

"I had some things to take care of this afternoon."

"Like?"

Did he really want to know she spent all afternoon getting a bank account, place to stay, and looking for a job? She shook her head.

"Do you have my bag?"

He nodded, "In my car."

He stood and gently took her hands. "Let's dance."

She shook her head again. She was craving that

feeling of last night. She wanted nothing more than to feel connected to someone again and she knew that was a problem. She had to focus on surviving now. Fun and games were over.

"Come on," he pled.

"I'm not in the mood."

"How can you not be in the mood for this?" He stepped back and gestured to his body as he salsa-ed. His hips swayed in time with the music in a corny, over-exaggerated way.

Alex lightly chuckled in spite of herself and Jason tried to pull her to her feet again, but she resisted.

"What's wrong?" he asked.

"Nothing."

He sat back down and stared deep into her eyes, "What's wrong?"

"I tried to get the Director to let me audition for the school. He said there was no way."

"Why not?"

"He said he couldn't get the whole committee together to watch me," she was getting choked up. "Can we just go get my stuff?"

"Really?"

She nodded and he slumped, defeated.

"Sure." He stood and motioned for Alex to follow him out. They walked to a nearby alley where Jason had parked his car. He strolled over to the driver's side and pulled out his keys. Alex made her way to the passenger side and looked at him expectantly. He didn't unlock the car.

"Why's this bag so important to you?" he asked.

"Open the door."

"It's just stuff."

"It's all I have," she responded.

"There's gotta be more to it than that."

"Let me have it." She circled the car to try and snatch the keys from him. He retreated around to the other side.

"Tell me the truth and I'll get it for you," he said, pointing through the window at the bag.

"It's none of your business." She started circling the car again.

"Tell me," he taunted, evading her again. "I told you my deepest, darkest secrets. It's only fair."

"Why are you torturing me?" She cried, giving up both physically and mentally. These past two days had taken a toll on her and she was exhausted. "What did I ever do to you?"

He paused, "Did you ever wonder what was missing? Like, you had this sense that there was supposed to be more, but you couldn't figure out what it was. How do you move through the world like that? Misunderstood. Misinterpreted. Misjudged."

She stood there just staring at him; frozen in time. She didn't know what to say, because she did know. She'd lived it for years and that's why she left.

He continued, "Then one day you're shot through, like electricity, pulse racing; blood burning through your veins. Or your heart stops, seizes when you see her profile, soft focus - flawless. You hear her laugh cutting through the cacophony of the world. The sparkle in her eyes mesmerizes you, like stars on a clear night; you lose yourself in their depth. And you realize, it's not *what* was missing... it was *who*."

They looked at each other in silence. The sounds of light traffic nearby and city life muted. The eyes of strangers passed them by under the hazy illumination of street lights.

Alex finally broke the trance. "You're good, poetic even, but sad," she sighed. "Like a puppy."

"Harsh," he play-acted like he'd been stabbed in the heart. "But I'm serious."

"You don't even know me."

"I'm trying to," he said. "But you won't let me."

"When I left home, I took everything that meant anything to me and I put it in my bag," she said. "That bag." She pointed into the car.

Jason unlocked his door and grabbed the bag.

"Like what?" He asked, holding the bag aloft and out of her reach. She met his eyes with a cold stare, not playing anymore.

"My mother is in there, okay?" she snapped. "Now let me have it."

Shock mixed with shame as Jason lowered the bag into Alex's hands, "I didn't..."

"It's her ashes," Alex continued as she cradled the backpack. "Well, some of them. I wanted to bring her here, to her home."

Jason climbed into the car, reached over and opened the passenger door.

"Get in," he said.

"Why?"

"Please?" He looked at her. "Trust me."

"Not tonight," she said. "I really need some time to think." She started off down the street, abandoning him just when he felt like he was making progress, again.

"You can't keep leaving me like this," Jason

called after her.

She looked back over her shoulder and held up her cell phone, "I've got your number."

∞∞∞∞

CHAPTER TEN:

Alex's new roommate had already gone for the

day as she relaxed at the table in their small kitchen

hunched over a bowl of Cheerios. She scrolled through

posts on her phone trying to find news from anyone she

had cared about back home when a knock at the door

shook her free from the screen. She padded over to the

front door, her bare feet slapping on the linoleum floor

and peered out of the peephole.

Outside, Jason rocked back and forth in slightly

nervous impatience. Alex quickly ran her hands through

her hair and checked if she had any stains on the old T-shirt and jeans she was wearing then cracked open the door.

"What are you doing here?" she asked.

"You didn't call," he smiled sheepishly.

"It's only been a two weeks."

"Funny," he said. "Feels like an eternity. Can I come in?"

She opened the door wider for him and he entered the small apartment. A worn love seat sat opposite a TV and an armchair that looked like a cat used it for a scratching post. Jason stood awkwardly just inside the doorway as Alex closed the door behind him.

"Nice place."

Alex rolled her eyes. "It's a place," she said. "How did you find me?"

"I know people, remember?" His confident charm returned and he unleashed his best Cheshire smile. "Plus, you're rooming with a dancer at the school." She chuckled and hit him in the arm.

"Why did you *want* to find me?"

"You've been on my mind. Every day since you took off on me. I have an idea."

She looked at him expecting more of an answer, but when none came she prodded him, "What was your idea?"

"I want you to come with me," he said. "On a boat."

"I can't." she responded, a little too quickly.

"Come on."

"I have to work."

"No today you don't," he said. "I asked around. This is your day off."

"I picked up an extra shift," she replied. "Good coffee waits for no man."

"You're lying," he teased her. "Just come with me. Please."

"I've never been on a boat," Alex confessed.

"Well, pack a bag and let's go then."

"I don't even have a swim suit."

He grinned broadly. "This is Miami. There are swimsuits on every corner," he said. "I'll buy you one."

Alex felt like she really could use a break. Plus, it was nice to see Jason and his self-assuredness again, even if it was a front half of the time. She needed a friend and she did like him. So she gave in and agreed to go.

Alex watched the highway as it slipped past the small hole in the floor of Jason's car. The motor seemed to be straining as they entered a brief stretch of highway.

"Is this thing going to explode?" she asked.

He shook his head no as he chuckled. "I don't think so. At least it hasn't yet."

"You're kinda messed up. You know that?"

He laughed out loud in a short burst. "You're not the first person to tell me that."

"Where are you taking me?"

"To the marina," he said, then paused before

continuing, "Tell me about your mother."

"No."

"Tell me about your mother and I'll tell you where I'm taking you really."

Alex glared at him feeling suddenly betrayed, "You said we're going out on a boat."

"We are. Tell me about your mother."

Alex looked out the window of the car. She could see the water between the tall buildings as they passed by. "She loved the ocean. Said it brought her peace."

Alex's gaze became unfocused as she recalled memories she had all but forgotten. "She would sit on the beach and listen to the surf. Just sit and listen."

Jason nodded understanding as Alex continued, "She brought me here once when I was little. I remember, it was a family vacation or something and we came to the beach."

"Why didn't you stay here?"

"My dad's job is very specialized I guess. When

he got an offer to work in Hot Springs, he took it and we never left."

"You're from Arkansas?"

She nodded.

"What's he do?'

"He's a choreographer."

Jason laughed, "Your dad's a dance choreographer and you came here with no connections?"

Alex crossed her arms and slouched in her seat, "You don't understand."

"No, I get it," he said. "I'm sure Hot Springs doesn't have much of a ballet company."

"And no ocean," she said almost to herself.

Boats of all shapes and sizes gently rocked with the surf as they pulled in to the Biscayne Bay marina. There were million dollar yachts and there were small fishing charters, people of all walks of life sharing the water. Alex liked the idea of that. You could clearly see the social stratification, but they all had to share the water. No one owned that.

Jason parked and hopped out of the car, "Grab your bag."

"Which boat is yours?"

"None. My friend Markus' family has one and he said we could use it."

"You have a license or something?"

He smiled at her, "Doesn't everyone?"

She smiled back at him, "Of course you do."

They approached a smaller boat. It was nice, but no yacht. Just a typical three or four person cabin cruiser named *Eternity Rising*. Still, it was more boat than Alex had ever been on.

A young guy with a healthy tan was moving things around on board and Jason quickly hopped up and gave him a hug. Then he turned and offered Alex a hand to climb on board.

"Alex, this is Markus."

She shook his hand.

"He's a dancer at the school too."

"Are you coming with us?" she asked.

Markus shook his head, "I wish, but no. I've got classes this afternoon." He turned to Jason, "Everything's ready. I'll untie you and you can take off. Just be careful, huh?"

Jason gave Markus his most self-assured smile and handshake, "Thanks brother. I owe you one."

"I'll just add it to your tab then?"

They half-hugged each other and Markus hopped onto the dock and untied the boat for them. "You're all set," he called as he made his way down the dock. Alex watched him go as Jason started the boat. She quickly grabbed a handrail as the floor beneath her started to move and they slowly backed out of the dock.

The sun bounced off of the water as they travelled across the gentle swells of the bay. Alex sat looking out at the peaceful ocean. She could see why her mother loved it so much. There was a rhythm to the water, a grace to the way it moved, a beauty that reflected the world around it. She felt like she was part of a larger dance out there - something bigger than herself. But she still felt connected. She could smell it. Feel it. Hear it. She turned to Jason as he steered the ship with purpose. She smiled, but he didn't see her, "Thank you," she whispered.

He turned and smiled back at her, "Almost there."

She didn't know where there was, but she didn't want to get there. Not yet. She just wanted to be part of this longer. Before she could finish her thoughts, Jason cut the engine. Alex looked around. They were floating in the middle of open water. She didn't see anything nearby. No land. No other boats.

"Where are we?"

"Look down."

Alex leaned over the rail and looked beneath her.

The water was shallower than she'd imagined, maybe forty feet, and she could see things on the floor of the ocean beneath them. There were stone sculptures, ornate columns, and sea life. "What is this place?"

"It's a celebration of life. They built this underwater cemetery where people could bury their loved ones."

Alex frowned as she thought about burying someone underwater.

"Bury isn't the right word," Jason continued. "People put their loved ones here, their ashes. The structures are intended to help the sea life grow and be sustained, like a man-made reef. Then the people can come out here and visit, be a part of the life springing up in the water."

"It's nice."

"Go get your suit on," he motioned towards the cabin. "I'll get the gear ready."

"What gear?"

Jason and Alex sat on the back of the boat, ready to take the plunge into the water. They wore snorkeling masks and flippers. Alex was nervous. She couldn't recall ever swimming in something so vast or deep; or unpredictable. She could see ocean life under the water, abundant and free, but she also knew there was danger in that life. It could be hiding, waiting for its chance.

Jason did his best to re-assure her, "Just remember, if you go under, when you come back up blow the water out of your snorkel before you inhale. If there's anything dangerous, I'll get you out. Ready?"

He dropped into the water, emerged and looked back at Alex, "Come on."

She dropped in and followed Jason's lead. Soon she was confident enough with her snorkel that she could take everything in and enjoy her surroundings.

The sunlight broke through the water casting ribbons of light and shadow on the sand that moved and glistened. They swam towards a lion sculpture that was positioned at what could be considered the entrance. She marveled at the life growing on the stone and how the sculpture had become a part of this underwater world.

They passed structures that housed the remains of loved ones. They swam between columns and past memorials designed to resemble the beauty of the mythic city of Atlantis. Schools of fish danced around them, some bolted before she could focus on them, startling her; she only noticed the sand that they kicked up as they scattered across the ocean floor. Sponges and coral grew around and on the stones that were placed there.

They swam for what felt like hours, surfacing and diving or just swimming above it. She was lost in the beauty of it all until Jason motioned for them to return to the boat.

They climbed aboard and pulled off their masks and snorkels. Alex squeezed water out of her hair as they dangled their feet in the water.

"Well?" Jason asked.

"It's beautiful. Peaceful," she said. "Thank you for bringing me here."

He shrugged, "I thought you might like it. You brought your bag, right?"

She looked at him not quite understanding where he was going with this, "Yeah..."

He nodded towards the water, "You wanna?"

"Want to what?"

"You know, return your mother to the sea."

Alex was shocked and she let him know, "You thought you'd bring me here and I'd spread my Mom's ashes in the water?"

He nodded feeling a little too sheepish to respond. Maybe this wasn't a good idea after all.

"It's not like I carry them with me everywhere I go."

"They were in your bag."

"Because I didn't have any place to stay yet," she said. "I had everything in my bag. And you thought you'd bring me out here and I'd just suddenly let her go?" She was really angry and she wasn't sure why. Why did the thought of spreading her mom's ashes in the ocean make her so... scared? Like she would be gone for real and Alex would be alone. She knew that Jason thought this would be a nice thing he could do for her, a good thing. But for some reason it just felt presumptuous and naïve, "Do you have any idea what it's like to lose someone?"

He shook his head slowly and couldn't meet her eyes, "You said she loved the ocean."

Alex sighed, he was right after all, her mother had loved the ocean. She spoke to herself as much as she spoke to him, "You don't understand. Your parents are perfect. You have everything anyone could want. Why would you get it?"

"Nothing's perfect."

"Oh, that's right," she snapped. "You don't like ballet, but you're too scared to admit it. That must be hard."

Jason was tired of getting beat up and his frustration took over, "I'm trying to help you."

"I didn't ask for your help. I'm not broken in a

way that you can fix," she said. "I have to fix it."

"But you don't have to do it alone."

"Yes, I do." That was exactly how she felt – alone. She stood up and disappeared into the cabin of the boat. After a moment of watching the water lap against the hull, Jason climbed to his feet, started the boat, and piloted them back to dock in silence.

∞∞∞∞

CHAPTER ELEVEN:

On the way back to Miami, they rode in silence

and Alex once more stared at the ground zipping by

beneath her through the hole in the car's floor. They

hadn't really spoken other than formalities. Alex wasn't

mad, not really. She just felt alone. She didn't have any

friends here. No family. Jason seemed like the only one

who wanted to get to know her at all. And he didn't get it.

He couldn't.

"I'm sorry," Jason finally broke the tension that

had built between them. "I didn't understand. I don't

know what it's like. But I want to."

She looked over at him. "No you don't. No one should know what it's like to lose their mother."

"No, not that..." he stammered. "I want to know how you feel. No, I don't want to know how you feel. I mean, I want to know how you're feeling... about everything. I want to be there for you. Here, I want to be here for you." He palmed his face as he struggled to find the right words. His difficulty was refreshing and endearing to Alex and she felt the tension leaving her body as she relaxed. Maybe he was who she'd hoped he was.

"I get it," she gave him a small smile. "Now watch the road, you're drifting."

He steered back into the center of his lane. "I really do want to help you."

She nodded.

"And I think I know a way to get you seen by the committee," he said.

"What are you talking about?"

"School. The Director said you need to be seen

by the whole committee before you can get admitted, right?" he said. "Well, I've been thinking about it all week."

"But he said no. And your mother couldn't even help get me a look."

"I know. But every year the school hosts a student showcase for all the local dance companies. The students in it have to do everything. Music selection, choreography, lighting, dancing. I've never done it before."

"And?" Alex's curiosity was piqued as she began to see where he was going with this.

"This separates the dancers from the choreographers, the administrators from the artistic directors. It gives everyone a chance to find their niche."

"And the whole staff watches," Alex finished for him practically bursting.

"You stole my thunder," he accused her. "But yes, that's the general idea. And you could be my partner for the showcase."

Alex sank back in her seat. "But I'm not a student."

"The students are in charge, remember. I'm in charge of my performance. I pick who I dance with. But there is one condition." He looked grave. "We don't do ballet."

"But it's a ballet school," Alex protested.

"I don't want to dance ballet, remember."

"But, I do."

"I know, but this is my showcase as much as a chance for you," he said. "They'll see you dance. They'll watch your technique. It'll work... I think."

She paused and turned away from him to take a moment to reflect on the opportunity. The light clouds in the clear, blue sky seemed to dance in a gentle breeze as the car sped down the highway. The world was full of hope, for the first time in a long time. She could see a future. Maybe it would work. This could be everything she'd been searching for. A way in. A way to honor her mother.

She turned to him, "Where could we practice?"

"The Pendulum. I bet I can get the space when they're not open during the day. They like me."

She grinned at him as the pieces began to fall into place, "What's not to like?"

He smiled back, "Plus, I have to do it this year so I can graduate."

"Why do I suddenly feel like I'm being played again?"

"I'm not playing you," he laughed. "But I am getting something I want out of it."

"What's that?"

"To dance with you again," he said.

She punched him in the arm.

He put his hands up in surrender. "But you get seen by all the right people."

"How long do we have?"

"A few months. It's a Christmas showcase."

"That's not much time."

He nodded and smiled triumphantly, "We better get started."

∞∞∞∞

CHAPTER TWELVE:

*T*he Pendulum was a different place during the

day. Gone was the loud music. Sweaty bodies under hot

lights were no longer on display. The cold concrete floor

was swept clean and the tables all had their chairs

stacked on them upside down. And it was bigger than

Alex had realized any other time. As far as practice

spaces went, this one worked.

She and Jason stood in the center of the dance

floor staring at each other awkwardly until she finally

broke the silence, "So, what did you have in mind?"

He shrugged and smiled at her, "I haven't gotten

that far yet. Any ideas?"

"You don't even have an idea?" She asked, "Not one?"

He shook his head. "The only reason I'm doing this is for you."

"You're doing this for me?"

He nodded.

"Not so you can graduate and get free from your parents expectations?"

He ran a hand through his hair and looked at the ground.

"Fine. Then let's put on some music."

He looked at her as she strode over to the bar and powered the sound system on. She hit play and a hot, Latin rhythm spilled forth from the speakers.

"That's better." She strode toward him allowing her hips to sway as she placed one foot in front of the other until she was within arm's reach. She put her hand on his chest and started to push him backwards. He moved with her for a moment, then pushed back. Her arm gently collapsed and they were pressed against each other. Their legs stepped in sync, but they kept their hands off of one another. Their faces were so close together they could feel each other's breath on their skin. Eyes locked together, they moved across the floor. Jason inched closer and their lips brushed as Alex turned her head to the side.

She put a finger across his lips as his hands found her waist and slid down to her hips. He spun her, caught her close, and pulled her across the floor. She caressed his face until he turned and began to walk away. A few more steps and she leapt onto his back, wrapping her arms and legs around him.

They spun together. They stalked each other. They flew through the air in magnificent leaps. Glistening with sweat and out of breath, they sat on the concrete floor. Jason's fingers rested atop Alex's and he looked into her eyes, drinking in every bit of her. She felt herself getting lost in his gaze; enraptured. She took a deep breath, "That seems like a good start."

He nodded.

"Let's take a little break then get back to it."

"We can do more tomorrow," he said.

She smiled at him and shook her head. "This has to be perfect. And we don't have much time."

"What did I get myself into?"

Alex stood and pulled Jason to his feet.

"Again," she commanded.

"I need a little more of a break than that," he protested. "Fifteen minutes?"

"Again."

He sighed and took up his starting position as Alex hit play one more time.

∞∞∞∞

CHAPTER THIRTEEN:

Lidia and José sat at their dining room table

playing a game of cards as Jason attempted to sneak into

the house passed them. He marveled at how his parents

could just enjoy being with each other without really

doing anything. He wondered if that was what it was like

to be old. If it was, then he didn't want to be old... unless

it was with Alex. He paused and wondered why that idea

just popped into his brain. He looked at his parents once

more. They were content, happy even. He shook his head

as he crept by, hoping they wouldn't notice him.

"Where have you been all day?" asked Lidia

without taking her eyes off of her cards.

"Out."

"You weren't in school," José mentioned casually as he drew a card.

"I was practicing for the Christmas showcase."

José and Lidia both put down their cards and looked at him.

"You entered?' his mother asked.

He nodded.

"Are you doing a solo?"

He shook his head, "I have a partner."

"Is it Joy?" asked José.

Jason shook his head, "Alex."

Lidia raised an eyebrow.

"Don't give me that look, Mom," Jason said.

"What look?"

"That one," he said, "the one that says surprise and suspicion all wrapped up together."

"Well, you've just never entered the showcase before."

"I know."

José patted his wife's hand as he spoke to his son, "You look tired."

Jason nodded, "Exhausted."

José nodded towards the bedrooms and Jason quickly disappeared. Lidia glared at her husband after their son had vanished.

"Why'd you let him go?" she demanded playfully.

"Don't interrogate the boy," he answered. "Be glad he wants to graduate. Even if it's for a girl."

"That's what I'm worried about... the girl."

José nodded, "I know."

"He doesn't have a great track record of things holding his interest for very long," she said. "Especially relationships. And Alex is... fragile."

"I know."

"Remember what happened when he dated Joy?"

"I know. We don't need to go over it again."

"I don't think he even wants to be a dancer anymore."

"I know."

"Then why'd you let him go?"

"Because he's our son," answered José. "And he's tired."

"So am I," said Lidia.

"I know," said José as he patted her hand again.

∞◌◌∞

CHAPTER FOURTEEN:

Alex rested on her bed looking out the window

at the moon and the stars. She was worn out after

dancing all day with Jason, but they were making good

progress. She was just worried it wouldn't be enough.

She rolled over and looked at the picture of her

mother from the Miami City Ballet on her night stand.

"This is what you wanted, isn't it?" she asked.

"Well, I'm doing it. I wish you were here. I even wish dad

was here." She sighed, "I wish he never sent you that

message. Then you'd have been looking at the road

instead of your phone and you would be here. And he

would be here too. I miss you... I miss you both."

     She thought about calling her dad. Just picking up the phone and dialing. She wondered if he'd even answer. If he even cared where she was or what she was doing. She wiped away the tears that streaked down her cheeks, rolled over, and stared at the moon again; lost in thoughts about what could have been until sleep overtook her.

∞∞∞∞

CHAPTER FIFTEEN:

*T*he Pendulum reverberated as Jason and Alex

swayed to the beat. He moved her hips as she leaned into

him. He dragged her across the floor. She leapt onto his

back. They caressed each other's faces. They spun. They

kicked. They flew through the air; synchronized

perfectly. Dust caked on their bodies mixed with sweat

as Jason collapsed to the floor in exhaustion. His hair

dripped and he breathed deeply and heavily.

Alex looked at him, "What are you doing?"

"Taking a break."

"We have work to do."

"We've been at it non-stop for a week," he said. "How about we have some fun for a change?"

"I thought you liked dancing with me?"

"I do. But, I just think we need a break," he said. "Enjoy ourselves a little."

"I don't have the luxury of fun right now."

"You've got this already."

"It's not enough," she said. "I have to stand out. Be spectacular. I have to make them notice me."

"They're already going to notice that we're not doing ballet."

"That's part of the problem," Alex said. "I need to add some ballet. Something really difficult, like a Butterfly into a Fouetté."

"That's impossible."

She put her hands on her hips and glared at him. "Then I'll do a Kitri's Grand Jeté."

"Can you even do that?"

"I can do a Bournonville Grand Jeté," replied

Alex. "I've done that before."

"You're pushing too hard already," said Jason as he sat up.

"What am I supposed to do?" asked Alex. "This is everything. If I don't show them what I'm capable of then they won't take me."

"I'm taking a break." Jason climbed to his feet, snatched a towel and threw it over his head as he downed a water bottle on his way out the door. Alex watched him go then threw her arms up in frustration.

"Fine."

She marched to one side of the dance floor and got a running start. She leapt into the air and did the splits curling her rear leg to her head as she arched her back. She stumbled as she tried to land on one foot.

Frustrated with herself, she marched to the side of the dance floor again. She got a running start and leapt into the air. He split was perfect and she had tremendous height. She landed on her front leg with her rear foot curled up to her head behind her; perfect... for a millisecond. Then her world exploded.

Her knee didn't hold her and, crying out, she fell to the floor in agony. She tried to stand up, but fell again in tremendous pain. Her leg would not support her. It was bent at an unnatural angle at the knee and felt numb. Jason rushed in after hearing her cry and immediately knew something was dreadfully wrong.

∞∞∞∞

CHAPTER SIXTEEN:

Alex woke in a sterile white room at Mercy

hospital. An IV provided fluids and pain killers while a

large brace immobilized her left leg. She tried to shift her

body and winced as the sensation of thousands of

electric needles shot through her knee.

Jason knocked on the doorframe as he entered

the room. He carried her bag loaded with her personal

items. She smiled as he approached and passed her

things to her.

"Thanks."

Jason sat in a chair next to the bed.

"I'm glad to see you're more with it," he said. "You were loopy on pain killers when they brought you in. I thought you'd lost your mind."

"Did I say anything weird?"

He nodded, "You said I was the most beautiful horse you'd ever seen. You called me a stallion."

She smiled and laughed lightly.

"I appreciate you getting my stuff."

"What'd the doctor say?"

Alex struggled to control her voice, "She said I dislocated my knee and tore some ligaments."

"What does that mean?"

"It means... with surgery I should be able to walk again in a few months."

Jason smiled, "That's good." He seemed genuinely excited and Alex started to get annoyed at his joy over her pain. She broke down in tears then. Tears that had been a long time coming.

Jason moved to comfort her and slipped his arm

around her shoulders. "What's wrong?"

"She said I'll never dance again." Alex sobbed. Her life was over. Dancing was all she knew. It was who she was and now it was gone too. But worst of all, she'd let her mother down.

"Look," said Jason, "if you can walk then you can dance. We'll get through this together."

Alex shook her head, "If I put any stress on it then it could dislocate again. And that's if it heals right. And it could happen again and again and again. Even with surgery and they're going to do that the first thing tomorrow."

"That soon? Do you want me to stay with you tonight?"

Alex shook her head, "I'll be fine."

"I'm going to stay."

"No, you need to find another partner."

Jason was stubborn in his refusal, "You can't make me go. You can't even get up." He backed away from the bed and put his hands in the air. "See. Come get me."

Alex threw a pillow at him which he caught. He returned to her side, "I'm not leaving you."

"You won't be able to graduate."

"I'm going to tell you a secret," he said as he leaned forward towards her ear. "I don't care," he whispered as he kissed her cheek.

Alex choked back a new round of tears as she wrapped her arms around him in a desperate hug. Her injury wasn't life threatening, but she was fighting for her life in that moment and Jason was her anchor.

Lidia sat in the chair in Alex's room. A small light illuminated the book that she was reading while Alex slept. A nurse entered to check on Alex and as she did so, Alex stirred awake. She groggily looked around the room for Jason, but instead found Lidia sitting in the chair.

"Lidia?' she asked.

Lidia moved closer to Alex and whispered, "Hey, sweetie."

"What are you doing here? Where's Jason?"

"Jason didn't want to tell me what was going on, but I could tell something was wrong. So, I made him."

"Where'd he go?"

"He's in the lobby," Lidia said. "He wouldn't leave even when I told him I needed to talk to you privately."

"I like him."

"Me too. He's a good kid." She took Alex's hand and held it. "He told me about his plan to get you in front of the committee and how you pushed so hard."

Alex struggled to hold it together, "But it's all gone now. I'll never be who she wanted me to be."

Lidia wrapped Alex in a motherly embrace. "Oh, honey. Parents only want the best for their children. She never meant it to be a burden. She wanted to see you soar."

"I'll never soar again."

Lidia leaned back, "Do you remember my cats?"

Confusion played across Alex's face and Lidia picked up on it. "The cats in my office."

Alex nodded.

"I'm allergic to cats. I'll never own one, but I still surround myself with them. They're still a part of my life. And I still love everything about them," she said. "Do you understand?"

Alex nodded again.

"Now, you go back to sleep. You've got a big day tomorrow. You'll need your strength."

"Will you stay with me?" Alex asked.

Lidia nodded. "I'll be here the whole time."

"Promise?"

"I promise."

Lidia patted Alex's hand and started to gently rub it as Alex closed her eyes. She quickly fell back into a deep sleep. She had found people who cared and that brought her a sense of peace that she hadn't had in a long time.

Alex woke and found her room empty. She wiped at her blurry eyes and looked around in near panic until Lidia walked in carrying a cup of coffee. Alex relaxed when she saw her.

"I thought you left me."

"I'm sorry. They told me you wouldn't be up yet, so I grabbed a cup of coffee," Lidia said. "But I'm here and I'm not going anywhere. Jason's still here too if you want to see him"

Alex nodded, "Did the doctor talk to you?"

Lidia shook her head. "She couldn't until you gave her permission. But I overheard them saying that everything went well."

"Did they say if I'll be able to walk again?"

"They didn't..." her voice trailed off as she was hesitant to share some more information. But Alex could tell something was amiss.

"What is it?" she asked. "What aren't you telling me?"

Lidia patted her hand. "Another time."

"Is it about my leg?"

Lidia shook her head.

"Then tell me."

Lidia took a deep breath, "I called your father."

Alex about leapt out of the bed. Emotions fought for control. Anger. Shock. Curiosity. "Why did you do that?"

"He's your father," she said. "It was the right thing to do."

Alex folded her arms and sunk into her bed, "He didn't even care, did he?"

"I didn't get to talk to him."

"Figures," Alex fumed. "Probably wasted on the couch again."

"Alex. Your father died of an overdose a few

weeks ago."

Alex fought to contain her emotions once more. This was too much. She'd hated him, what he'd become, but she never wanted him dead. She didn't really never want to see him again. She just couldn't bear the pain she felt every day looking at him. He was her father after all.

"He's dead?" She sounded like a small child. She felt like a small child. Alone and afraid. She looked at the ceiling and swallowed back tears. "I don't know why I'm crying," anger now kept her going. "He died to me the night my mother died. It was all his fault anyway."

Lidia moved closer to her.

"I told him when I left. I told him I hated him." Alex couldn't hold in her grief and guilt any longer. Lidia embraced her.

"I told him I hated him."

"He was your father and no matter what, he loved you," said Lidia. "And he knew you loved him."

It was all too much. Alex couldn't bear the pain.

Her whole body felt numb. She wished her mind would just go numb as well. She'd left, but there was always hope, deep down, that her father would come back to her. That he'd see her dance and come back. That she might remind him of her mother and he'd remember that there was a reason to live. There was hope, but not anymore.

She cried until there were no more tears left and her throat and eyes were raw from grief. She'd failed her mother and now she'd failed her father too.

She held Alex in her arms until, exhausted, she mercifully fell into a deep sleep.

∞∞∞∞

CHAPTER SEVENTEEN:

*J*ason pushed Alex in a wheelchair through the parking lot of the hospital as the Miami sun warmed her soul and lifted her spirits a little. Crutches rested across her lap as he propelled her towards his car. It had been a few days since news of her father had left her absolutely broken; separated. No surgery was going to help her heart heal. But then there was Jason. He hadn't left the hospital for more than a shower in the days that she had been cooped up there. What stability she felt was because of his constant presence.

"I can use the crutches you know," she said.

"The doctors said the more you stay off of your leg the better, right?" he said. "Plus, this is more fun."

Alex sighed, then giggled, as he spun through the rows of parked cars like a drift racer until they arrived at his. It was good to laugh.

She climbed to her feet using the crutches, like they'd showed her in physical therapy, after Jason had locked the wheels on the chair. It wasn't easy. Recovery was going to be hard and take a while. Jason ran to open the car door for her.

"Now you're opening doors for me?" she teased. "I should've crippled myself sooner."

"Nah," he smiled back at her, "I just figured if you're going to be staying in the same house as me we'd better get started off on the *right* – I mean *left* foot." He giggled at his bad pun and Alex rolled her eyes.

"Funny."

"Because your leg is-"

Alex cut him off. "I get it," she said. "Just don't repeat it."

Alex glanced back at the hospital before ducking into the car and starting to fasten her seatbelt. As Jason struggled to find a way to get the wheelchair into the vehicle she was surprised by the memory of her mother in the hospital, just after the accident.

She'd gone with her father and when he'd left the room she stood next to her mother. Tubes protruded from her mouth, arms, and nose. Her pulse beat on the machines that were keeping her alive, but she wasn't awake. Wasn't aware. Alex squeezed her hand. No response.

"Mom, wake up," she begged. "It's me, Alex."

Just a slow beeping in the background answered her.

"I need you to be okay. If I'm going to be a dancer like you I need you to help me," she cried. "And for that, you need to be here."

The memory faded as her mother had throughout that night until they were both no more.

Alex's grief had caught her by off guard, she was unaware that something so simple might trigger it. Maybe it was because she was feeling so vulnerable and helpless right now. Overwhelming sadness pushed on her no matter how hard she tried to put it out of her mind.

She thought about all of the good things that were happening. In the midst of this crisis, Lidia and José had offered her their guest room until she was able to get back on her feet, literally. It was like she had a new family. And Jason was sweet, attentive. She really liked him and he seemed to really like her. But what if "living together" made them feel more like brother and sister? She didn't want that. She wanted romance. She wanted to be the dancer who was dating the passionate poet who acted from his heart instead of his head. What if that went away now too?

She was silent as he got in and started the engine.

"You okay?" he asked.

She nodded and he patted her hand... he patted her hand. She knew it was supposed to comfort her, but it just seemed to confirm what she was thinking and she had to look out of the window to avoid bursting into tears again. Great, she'd gone from never wanting to cry to being the girl who cried all the time. Not optimal relationship material.

"Just thinking about my dad," she lied.

Jason nodded and pulled out, heading home.

Lidia stood in the doorway of her guest room watching Alex gently sit on the bed and lean her crutches on the wall next to her. Alex looked around the room. There was a dresser with a mirror like the one she had back home, the bed, and a nightstand with a small lamp and a cat figurine. Alex picked up the feline; it was a black and white tuxedo cat playing with a pickle. She chuckled.

Lidia smiled. "I thought he could keep you

company."

"Thanks," said Alex. "I really appreciate you letting me stay here."

"There were times, when I was dancing, that I needed people to be there for me," replied Lidia. "Your mother was always the first to help. And we just want to see you back on your feet."

Alex groaned and rolled her eyes, "You too? There's got to be something genetic with the humor."

Lidia feigned shock, "What?"

"You and Jason and the corny jokes." Alex chuckled as did Lidia.

"You remind me so much of your mother. It will be a pleasure to have you around," said Lidia. "Plus, we could talk about girl things. I never had a girl in the house to share with." She smiled at Alex with affection.

Jason arrived behind Lidia, pushing the empty wheelchair. "Come on, Mom. You're going to scare her away," he said. "This already has to be weird enough."

Lidia stepped aside so Jason could get into the room.

"Thanks." Said Alex as he parked the chair beside the bed.

"You need anything just let me know."

"I will, thanks."

Lidia put her hand on her son's shoulder as she spoke to Alex, "Why don't we let you get settled in some before dinner."

Alex nodded and the two left. She sighed heavily and looked out the window at the clear blue sky. Miami skies were always clear and blue she thought. The sun cast its rays into her room and everything seemed a little bit brighter. She pulled the photo of her mother out of her bag and placed it on the nightstand, next to the cat.

"This isn't quite what we expected, is it?"

Alex tried to stand and winced in pain. She hopped on one foot over to the wheelchair and plopped down into it. She ran her hands down the arms and onto the wheels for a spin.

"Looks like we're partners for a while," she said. "I guess we should get used to each other." She spun the chair around the bed and sat at the window, letting the sunlight splash down on her.

∞∞∞∞

CHAPTER EIGHTEEN:

*J*ason crept into Alex's room as she sat in her

wheelchair staring out at the sunset. She seemed

oblivious to his presence, so he gently cleared his throat.

She turned her attention to him and mustered up a sad

smile.

"Hey," he said.

"Hey."

"What're you doing?"

"Thinking."

"About?"

She hesitated, "Nothing."

He frowned and sat on the edge of her bed so he could be eye level with her. "You haven't left this room for more than a meal for a few days now," he said. "Do you not like it here?"

"It's not that." She shook her head. She knew he wouldn't understand, couldn't understand. Her mom was gone. Her dad was gone. She was an orphan now. And she thought that should somehow change her world, but it didn't. She thought she was supposed to be wracked with grief, but she wasn't. Nothing had changed really and that made her... sad.

"You've been alone in here for too long."

"I've been alone for a lot longer than the few days I've been in here," she answered. "It's nothing new."

"But you're not alone," he protested. "I'm here. My mom and dad are here."

Alex smiled at him, "That's just it. *Your* mom and dad. Not mine."

"What about me?'

"I'm still not sure if you're just playing me." She smiled at him as he chuckled.

"It's time."

"Time for what?" she asked.

"To move on. Move forward with life."

"That's what I was doing," she said. "Then this happened." She gestured at her chair and her injured leg.

"So?" he scorned. "Your life isn't over."

"But everything I lived for is gone," she shot back. "What do you do when everything comes crashing down at once? What have you ever lost? I don't even know why I'm doing this. What's the point?"

She was letting him in further than she'd ever let anyone. She wasn't comfortable being this vulnerable. She felt helpless and needy. And she hated it.

He looked at her, the tears brimming in her eyes that she wouldn't let free. "Duck and cover?" He answered with a silly grin. "Like they teach you in elementary school when a tornado's coming." He put his hands over the back of his head and hid his face with his elbows, hoping to lighten the mood.

It didn't work as Alex seemed exasperated, "That's what I'm doing."

He nodded, "You need to figure things out. Settle with your past. I can't answer your questions for you. That's something you have to wrestle with. But I can help you in one way, pack your bag. We're going on a road trip."

"Where to?"

"Hot Springs."

She nodded and knew he was right. She had to face the past in order to move beyond it. She needed to go home... one last time. But she was afraid of what she might find. What if she discovered that her life really was meaningless? Or worse, what if she got stuck in the past and Jason left her there? Her insecurities mounted as she contemplated what she had to do next and she turned away from Jason towards the window once more.

"Why do you want to help me now? I don't have

anything to offer anymore."

He moved to her and placed his hand on her shoulder. "It was never about what you could do for me." The warmth of his touch nearly broke her as she struggled to swallow the emotions rising up inside. She hadn't felt like she mattered to anyone in years, but Jason made her feel like she was special. Like she was wanted. "It was always about what we could do together."

She sighed heavily, "When do we leave?"

∞∞∞∞

CHAPTER NINETEEN:

Alex and Jason spent hours in the car the next

day. The sun beat down gently as the wind breezed in

through the open windows. The weather was a

counterpoint to the storm that brewed inside Alex. She

felt light as she reclined in her seat, but she knew the

heaviness was coming. This wasn't a vacation that she

was on. She was travelling to claim her father's ashes and

take care of what property had been left behind. Not

your typical, carefree, 18 year-old stuff. But she wanted,

more than anything, to be a carefree, 18 year-old.

Jason took a detour towards Talladega National Forest. He knew it was a little out of the way, but he had a plan.

"Where are you going?" Alex asked.

"I want to show you something."

She sat up attentively as she tried to discern their destination. After a short while, she noticed signs for the park.

"I can't really go hiking."

Jason smiled, "I know."

He pulled in to a parking spot at the park and helped Alex climb out of the car. They didn't travel far before they came to a sign that read, *Chinnabee Trail.*

"Do you know anything about this trail?" He asked her.

She shook her head.

"Boy Scouts built this trail," he said. "Deaf Boy Scouts."

Alex expected there was more to it than that, so

she waited until he continued.

"The troop leader, Moran Colburn, was a deaf guy who became an All American football player for the Silent Warriors football team. Then he became Deaf Coach of the Year a little later. But more than that, he spent over 30 years as the coordinator for the Indian Dance Team."

"And you're telling me this because…"

"It's inspiring," he exclaimed. "Just think about it. This guy did all this stuff and he couldn't hear. He coached dancers and couldn't even hear the music."

"I'm not a Boy Scout."

"I know."

"I'm not handicapped either."

"Neither was he, clearly."

"I mean, I know I'm going to heal," she said. "But I can't dance anymore."

"That's why I brought you here. To show you that the only thing you really can't do, is give up."

He looked so excited to share this moment with her, but all she could think about was what she'd lost. She didn't want to crush his spirit, but that's what she did.

"I don't need a cheerleader," she spit out.

He was taken aback. This was not what he'd intended.

Her frustration with life and her situation burst out and she continued to lash him with her words, "I don't need to see all the great things other people did. I don't want my picture on an inspirational poster on some kid's wall."

"That's not—"

"It is," she laid into him. "It is exactly what you're doing. You're so optimistic and passionate about everything and I'm not." She didn't even have time to think before the words tumbled from her mouth, "I don't even know why you're helping me. You should just leave me here and forget I ever existed."

"I like you and I'm not leaving you here."

"Why? My life was one note and that was it."

"You're more than one note."

She shook her head, "I'm not though. *I* don't even know who *I* am anymore."

"I know who you are."

"You don't," she whispered. "You barely know me at all."

Jason stood in stunned silence. This had not gone well. In his mind, he'd pictured a whole different outcome. Maybe he really was trying to be a cheerleader, but he had wanted her to see that there was more to life than dancing. That she could do so much if she put her mind to it. Alex stood there helpless, looking lost, and his heart ached for her. He wanted to comfort her, to hold her. But he was at a loss too. He looked around for an escape or some way to lighten the mood without hurting her feelings. There wasn't one. The awkward silence persisted until Alex couldn't stand his pitiful stare anymore.

"Can we just go now?" she asked. "Please."

He nodded and they walked back to the car. He trailed behind her as she hobbled with her crutches on the unstable ground.

∞∞∞∞

CHAPTER TWENTY:

*T*he last time Alex had been in this funeral

home was for her mother's wake. She remembered all

the posters with pictures of her family, all the town's

people coming over to say they were sorry, the flowers...

but not today. Today the place was empty. It had this

smell, like mouthwash, that made her want to gag. She

almost turned and ran out, but Jason's hand on her

shoulder steadied her.

"Alex?" a woman's voice echoed through the

room and Alex turned around to see Mrs. Jones. She was

a plump woman, short, and in her mid-fifties. She

immediately embraced Alex in a familiar hug.

"I'm so sorry," she mumbled into Alex's chest then pulled back to arm's length and looked her over. "Nobody knew what happened to you. Some people thought you were dead. There were rumors."

Alex shook her head. "I was just in Miami trying to get into a company."

Mrs. Jones' eyes got big, "Did you make it?"

Alex looked at her leg and crutches, "It's been... things change."

Mrs. Jones nodded, "Are you going to take over your parent's studio then?"

Jason's head turned back and forth as the exchange continued. It was almost too much information for him to take in, the familiarity and half-finished thoughts left him confused.

"You wait here," Mrs. Jones said. "I have your father's ashes."

She disappeared and Jason turned to Alex, "You

know her?" He smiled playfully.

"Small town," Alex said. "I taught her daughters."

"Taught?"

"When my mom died I took over teaching the little kids. My dad taught the older ones."

Mrs. Jones returned with a cardboard box lined with a thick plastic. She looked solemnly at Alex and her crutches then handed it to Jason.

"What's this?" he asked.

"My dad." Alex replied, her tone completely flat.

Mrs. Jones nodded. "I'm sorry for your loss."

Jason looked at the box and at Alex. She was staring at the box as well, her affect had gone completely neutral.

"Thank you," she said to Mrs. Jones and started out on her crutches.

"I'm glad you're back," Mrs. Jones said. "I wish it were under different circumstances."

Alex nodded as she exited the building. Jason quickly followed. Mrs. Jones watched them leave and sighed as the door closed behind them.

∞∞∞∞

CHAPTER TWENTY-ONE:

*J*ason pulled his car into the driveway of a

small, brick house. The lawn was overgrown and a "For Sale" sign was planted in the middle of the front yard. He climbed out of the car and began to struggle with the wheelchair while Alex hobbled on her crutches to the front door. Her key still worked and she opened the door and stood for a moment taking in her old home.

Everything was where it had been. The couch, the coffee table, the recliner, but it was also so different. This wasn't her house anymore. She felt like a stranger here. It felt so empty.

She made her way to the recliner where she last saw her father, passed out. She traced her finger tips across the worn leather arm of the chair. "This is where he was the last time I saw him," she said. "When I told him good bye. And I hated him." She turned to the front door where she knew Jason was standing, watching. She turned back and moved further into the house, down the small hallway lined with joyful pictures of her family at various locations on vacations or dance trips.

She entered her room. It was exactly as she'd left it. She looked around at her belongings, her trophies that meant nothing now, her stuffed bear dressed like a ballerina that sat on her bed. Alex went over and picked the bear up, clutching it to her chest. She noticed her mother's old Bible sitting on her nightstand where she'd left it when she ran away. She paged through it, looking at her mother's hand written notes on every page. She'd been devoted. So had Alex, for a time. Then God took everything from her and she ran away.

Jason's voice gently broke the silence, "That

yours?"

She shook her head and closed the book. "My mother's."

"You believe in God?"

"I don't know anymore."

He nodded. "I get it."

"Do you?"

He nodded again. "You're not the only one who doubts."

"Yeah, well, I'm not sure I want to follow someone who took my parents from me."

Jason nodded, "I get that, too."

He ran a finger across her trophy shelf, "You have a lot of trophies," he said. "You must be a pretty good dancer." He grinned at her mischievously.

"There wasn't much competition."

"Yeah, I guess when both of your parents were professional dancers you can get a *leg up*."

Alex groaned, "My dad was a choreographer."

"He danced first though, right?" Jason asked. "He didn't start out as a choreographer. That happened later."

Alex nodded, "He was never the top of his class or anything, so his dance career was short lived."

"But he was a good choreographer?"

"He was," Alex said. "He could craft the most beautiful moments for me or my mother. That's why I won so many awards, not my dancing."

"Well, you had to be able to do the movements."

"I guess. But, all these trophies, achievements. What are they for?" She asked. "They don't mean anything. None of it means anything."

She plopped down on her bed and stared into space.

After a moment, Jason decided that maybe what Alex needed was some time to think. "Why don't I go get us some food? You get some rest."

Alex nodded and Jason disappeared. After a few

seconds she heard the front door close and she was alone, truly alone for the first time since she'd found out about her father's death. She looked to the doorway where Jason had been and her wheelchair peeked around the corner reminding her that this was all real. "Why are you doing this to me?" she cried.

She curled up into the fetal position on her bed and began to weep. She wept until exhaustion took her and she fell into a deep sleep.

Alex woke up in her bed, in her room, with the sun blazing through her window reflecting off of her trophies and she was confused. Her mother's Bible lay next to her and she put it back on the nightstand.

There were soft noises coming from the kitchen and she thought for a moment that everything that had happened over the last month had been a dream. She wished it was all a dream, but reality came crashing back for her as moved her leg and winced in agony. She shouldn't have been sleeping in that position for that long and her leg was stiff.

Rising to her feet, she made her way to the wheelchair and flopped into it. She wheeled into the kitchen and saw containers from a Chinese restaurant set on the table and Jason sitting with a pen making marks in a Cosmopolitan magazine.

"What are you doing?" she asked.

"Do you know how hard it is to find a Chinese restaurant around here?"

She smiled, "Are you reading Cosmo?"

"I already read it," he said. "You were asleep for a while. Now I'm doing the quizzes."

"Seriously?"

He nodded and smiled, "I haven't done these in years. I used to do them all the time when I was 14 or 15."

"But they're women's magazines."

"I always figured, what better way to know what girls want than to read their magazines." He chuckled,

"Then I'd take the quizzes to see how I was doing."

"You used them like a how-to manual?"

"Something like that."

"That's so sweet," she taunted playfully. "Were you a good boyfriend?"

"I'm filling this one in about you," he said. "You're doing terribly. Not a good girlfriend at all."

"Isn't it asking questions about having a boyfriend?"

He nodded, "Mmhmm."

"And I'm a girl. You know that right?"

He nodded again, "You're score is really low."

Alex laughed as she wheeled over to the table and began to serve herself some orange chicken. Jason took this as a cue and got himself some too. Alex shoveled a piece into her mouth realizing that he'd waited for her to get up and join him before he ate. He must have been starving, because as soon as she tasted the food she'd understood how hungry she was.

"So, the quiz is telling you that I'm not a good girlfriend?"

He nodded with his mouth full.

"I guess that makes sense, since I don't have a boyfriend." Her eyes sparkled as she spoke. Jason stopped his chewing and looked at her. He took a big swallow of food before speaking, "Maybe we should do something about that." He scooched his chair next to her and fed her another bite of chicken with his chopsticks.

"Like what?" she said as she finished the bite.

"We'll have to find you a boyfriend. There's gotta be someone around here who might be into you." They were all smiles as they played this game of cat and mouse. They got closer together, little by little.

"It's hard to find a decent guy in this town," she said. "Why do you think I left?"

"I thought it was because you wanted to be a dancer."

She shook her head, "I was just looking for a guy."

"I'm sure you didn't need to go all the way to Miami for that," Jason said. "Don't you have a bus station around here?"

Alex laughed out loud, "Miami's where the good ones are."

Jason smiled and stared deep into her eyes, "I'd really like to kiss you."

"I never kiss on the first date."

"We kinda already live together." He leaned in and pressed his lips against hers. She hesitated at first, but then gave herself over to the moment and melted. The kiss was soft and warm; tender. It was... luxurious. He gently cupped her face with one hand and, after he pulled away slightly, met her eyes with his.

"Will you be my girlfriend?" he asked.

"Maybe reading those magazines has paid off after all."

She leaned in and this time she kissed him with everything that was in her. She let this kiss restore her soul, giving herself over to the connection physically and emotionally. The world around her, her troubles, her pain, all vanished with his contact. She didn't want it to end. Ever.

The next afternoon, Jason pushed Alex through the small downtown of Hot Springs. Boutique shops lined the streets along with specialty restaurants. An historic hotel rested at the foot of a mountain next to a park and a little further down was a large window in a storefront where Alex and Jason paused. Through the window they could see a hard wooden floor, lines of mirrors, and a ballet bar mounted to a wall.

"This is it," Alex said.

"Looks nice. Should we go in?"

"In a minute." Alex stared through the glass at the empty dance school. Her parent's school. She'd spent the last few years running it by herself, trying to keep things afloat while her dad broke down. Every penny she brought in though, he'd spend escaping from reality. She remembered running here straight from high school each afternoon to teach ballet class to a roomful of little girls. As she looked at the empty studio now, she was sad.

"Okay, we can go in."

Jason opened the door and pushed her into the room. The wheels of her chair glided on the smooth wooden floor and she parked in the center, staring at herself in the mirror. Jason wandered over to a large stack of mail and started sorting through it.

"Looks like you've got a few bills here."

"I'm sure." She wheeled herself over to where he was and began sorting through the letters with him until they heard the door open. They both turned and looked as a 9 year-old girl with short blond hair tentatively stepped into the school.

"Miss Alex?" She asked.

Alex stared at her, trying to identify her against the sunlight pouring in.

"Sarah?"

The girl nodded then ran over and embraced

Alex, practically jumping in her lap.

"What happened?" Sarah asked.

"I was practicing my jumps and landed wrong."

"No. Why'd you leave us?"

Alex opened her mouth to answer, but couldn't think of anything to say. All her answers were selfish. She left to get away. To pursue her dreams. To honor a promise she made to her mother. But what about the promise she'd made to Sarah? To all the girls she'd been teaching? At that moment, Sarah's mother walked in.

"Sarah," she said, "Please wait for me outside."

Sarah climbed off of Alex and went back out front while her mother approached.

"I'm sorry about your father," she said.

Alex nodded, "Thank you."

"Are you going to be taking things over?"

"I..." Alex stammered. "I don't know."

"These girls missed you when you vanished. They didn't understand what happened. No one did.

Then the school closed down and many of their hopes and dreams with it." She squatted down to look Alex in the eye. "These girls look up to you. You're like family to them. It's not your responsibility to stay, but it is your responsibility to care about how you leave."

Alex nodded.

Sarah's mother stood and looked at Jason. "I hope you're taking good care of her."

He nodded.

"I'm sorry," Alex said.

"I know you are sweetheart. Take care of yourself." She turned and left.

Jason and Alex watched as she went out the door and took Sarah's hand. The two walked off together and Alex watched until they disappeared in the distance down the street.

The next morning, Jason entered Alex's bedroom as the sun dribbled through the blinds. He watched as dust pirouetted through the air towards the tray of food he'd prepared. He set it on her nightstand and looked at Alex. She looked peaceful, a contrast to the feelings he knew were battling inside her. He wished he could help her make the right decision as he gently brushed a few hairs off of her face. She stirred at his touch and cuddled into his hand as she slowly woke up. He watched her move and it made him happy. He looked on her with adoration. This girl. This pain-in-the-rear girl who he met at a bus station, who it seemed he had been destined to meet. He felt at peace in a way he'd never experienced before as he enjoyed the pressure of her face against his hand.

"We could stay here, you know," he said.

Alex stirred more, but had been half asleep when he spoke, "Hmmm?"

"We could stay here. You don't have to sell the house. We don't have to go back to Miami."

Alex woke more thoroughly now and sat up. She shook her head.

"We could run your parents' dance school," he continued. "Just us. You and me. Together."

Alex met his gaze, "This isn't my home. Not anymore," she said. "That was their dance school. Their life. Not mine."

"But we could do whatever we want. Be whoever we want to be. It's a fresh start."

"Not for me. Too many memories here."

"Then when the house sells, you'll have some money," he continued. "We could go somewhere new together."

As she looked at him, she could feel the longing in his heart. "Leaving isn't the freedom you think it is. You'll never be free until you tell your parents the truth. And running away isn't the answer."

"I don't want this to end."

"Then it won't," she said. "But we have things to take care of. Responsibilities. You have a student showcase to prepare for."

"But I don't have a partner anymore."

"What about Joy?"

He smirked, "Are you trying to get rid of me already?"

"She'd be your partner. I'm sure of it."

He nodded, "She would. Without hesitation. But I'm not looking for that kind of partner anymore."

"Oh, you know she wants you?"

"Who doesn't want this?" Jason moved his shoulders with a corny, exaggerated seductiveness. "She's been trying to get us together for years," he said. "I'm just not interested."

Alex detected a different vibe from Jason. He was making excuses, "You're afraid of her."

"I am not."

"You are," she taunted.

"Maybe a little," Jason laughed. "There could be some Fatal Attraction thing going on there. Plus, I like a girl who puts up a fight."

"You like the chase?"

"Only if the catch at the end is worth it."

Alex frowned, "I'm not much of a catch anymore."

"Let me be the judge of that." He leaned in for a kiss and she responded. Heat surged through their bodies as they wrapped their hands around each other, enfolded in an embrace. Jason pulled back for a breath, "Yeah, you're worth it."

Alex smiled, "You're not playing me, are you?"

Jason shook his head.

"So, what do we do now?" she asked.

He shrugged and kissed her again.

"This seems to work."

∞∞∞∞

CHAPTER TWENTY-TWO:

Alex wheeled into the kitchen where Jason sat

writing on some paper he'd found. He was so focused

that he didn't notice Alex come in, until she spoke.

"Whatcha doin'?"

"I was inspired to write a poem."

"But we're not in a bus station."

"I know, weird, right?" He smiled and put his

pen down.

Alex glanced at the paper with words scrawled

across it, scribbles, words slashed and replaced, arrows and circles. "You really work at it, don't you?"

Jason nodded.

"Can I read it?"

He shook his head, "You wouldn't be able to make heads or tails of it like this," he said. "But I'll read it to you."

He picked up the paper and cleared his throat, "Roses are red. Violets are blue-"

"Ha ha," Alex scoffed. "Seriously, let me read it."

"I was just warming up. This has to be done right."

He straightened his posture and held the paper in front of him so that it hid his face from hers. And he began...

"My mind is enchanted by God's greatest design,
She's fashioned in beauty and elegance refined.

Embraced by the joyous, rapturous sound,
Of angelic laughter unheavenly bound.

Spellbound I follow the brightest star in my sight,

She lights my way in the darkest of night.

Until gathered beneath the warm morning sun,
We tell of the stories not yet begun.

And hold forth a love that defines our life,
Enraptures our soul and conquers our strife."

"Wow," Alex said as she sat stunned for a moment, letting his words sink in. "You don't know me at all."

Jason smiled, "You liked it then?"

"I liked it. Though I think you're crazy."

"You wouldn't be the first."

Alex bit her lower lip as she worked up the courage to speak. She had been having such a wonderful time these past days with Jason that she didn't want it to end. But she knew it had to. They couldn't go on like this. Soon the reality of the world would intrude, uninvited and things would be miserable again. She couldn't stay here. He couldn't stay here. He'd be bored in no time and be dying to leave, but he'd never say it. No, it wouldn't be fair to him.

He could tell she was deep in thought about something and did what any good boyfriend should do, "What's up?"

"We have to go back."

"What are you talking about?"

"Miami. We have to go back."

"There's no rush." Jason shrugged.

"There is. You've got a showcase to do."

He shook his head, "That was for you. I don't care about that."

"I won't be the reason you don't graduate," she stared at him defiantly. "And I've been thinking... I know you don't want to do ballet. And I can't dance like this. Not in the traditional way at least."

"What do you mean, not in the traditional way?" Jason perked up. He loved a good challenge and was always up for something different.

"I was thinking about ice skaters and how they glide across the ice and they do these dance moves and jumps and throws. And, well, I can't jump. But this chair could glide."

"Wait a minute. You still want to be my dance partner?"

"I looked it up on Youtube," Alex explained. "People do it. Wheelchair dancing. And it's beautiful."

"Wheelchair dancing. Do I need to be in a chair too?"

She shook her head.

"But that won't get you into the school."

"Ever since my Mom died, I've focused only on only one thing; being who I thought she wanted me to be. Making her proud of me. But you know what I think would make her most proud?"

Jason waited.

"Not letting this define me. It's what happened to me, but it's not who I am. And it's not going to hold me back. And I'm going to help you be who you want to be. And for that, we need to go to Miami."

"You can't bring your mother back this way."

"I'm not trying to," she said. "I'm going to dance with you at your showcase so that everyone can see that there's more to who you are than ballet."

"By dancing in the showcase?" he said. "That seems a little backwards."

"Trust me. I have an idea."

∞∞∞∞

CHAPTER TWENTY-THREE:

Lidia sat at her desk, typing on her computer as

a soft knock disrupted her data input.

"Come in."

The door swung open and Jason pushed Alex in

her wheelchair into the office. Lidia's eyes lit up at the

sight of them and she leapt to her feet, crossed the room,

and had them in an embrace before Jason had fully

crossed the threshold.

"You're back!"

Alex smiled broadly.

"Hi, Mom," said Jason, his words muffled by her squeeze.

Lidia pulled away and wiped a tear from her eye.

"Are you crying?" asked Jason. "We were only gone a little while."

"I wasn't sure you were coming back." She moved aside so they could fully enter her office and close the door. "Were you able to take care of everything you needed too?"

Alex nodded.

"Almost," said Jason. "We weren't able to practice for the showcase."

"You're still going to do it? How? And you're running out of time."

"We know. But we don't have anywhere to practice anymore," he admitted. "They won't let us back where we were. Too much liability."

"We need your help," Alex said.

"What can I do?'

"Let us in, here. At night. When the studios aren't being used."

"But you're not a student. That's tricky."

"But, I am," said Jason. "And that's why we'd do it when no one's around. No questions."

"I'm not sure…"

"C'mon, Mom," Jason pleaded.

Alex begged with her eyes.

"I'm trusting you with my job here." Lidia sighed.

"We know. You won't regret it."

"Do I at least get to know what you're doing?"

Jason shook his head.

"We want it to be a surprise," said Alex.

Lidia took a deep breath, sighed heavily again and nodded.

∞∞∞∞

CHAPTER TWENTY-FOUR:

*T*he sun had set over Miami and the school

building was all but abandoned. Empty except for Alex

and Jason, who occupied a classroom with a full wall of

mirrors and smooth, wooden floor. The harsh

fluorescent lights reminded them of the cold assessment

they would receive at the showcase should their plans

fail. But they weren't about to give up.

A dark, hypnotic beat thrummed from the sound

system as Alex spun her chair rapidly until Jason caught

the handles and gave her a shove. The chair glided across

the floor. Jason ran after and, as Alex spun to face him,

he planted a foot on one arm and leapt high into the air. Alex watched the graceful arc as he crossed over her.

He twirled around the chair and executed a handstand with his legs split as Alex guided the chair through a slow circle. Then he returned to his feet only to collapse to the ground as the chair rolled over him, wheels passed by his sides and he rose behind Alex again and pranced towards her.

They continued for hours trying different movements and combinations; trying to find the right ones that would work. Jason lifted Alex from the chair and tossed her into the air where she twirled before he caught her clumsily. Over and over they attempted the move until they were both exhausted and took a break.

"We've been at this for weeks," she said as she gingerly climbed out of her chair and plopped down on the floor.

Jason grabbed their water bottles then sat next to her, "I know." He wiped the sweat from his face with his shirt. Alex couldn't help but notice his exposed six-pack.

"I can't say it hasn't been fun." She smiled at him and he returned the gesture.

"Not much longer and it will all be over," he said.

"How's your surprise coming along?"

He tapped his temple, "It's all here."

"I think we need some help. I can't do what I want to," Alex said. "We need another girl."

"You're doing fine."

She shook her head, "I'm not. I can't pull it off if I can't land. It's too much to expect you to be able to catch me after that."

"Then we do something else."

"No, we need to blow them away. Do something they've never seen," she said. "We need another girl."

"You know someone?"

She shook her head, "You do."

"Not this again."

She looked at him knowingly.

"Come on. You want me to ask Joy?"

"She'll do it for you."

"I know she will. And she'll hold it over me forever," he said, whining just a bit. "Do you know how many years I've avoided being her partner?"

"You should be nice to girls who like you."

"I am being nice, by not leading her on."

"I'm not asking you to lead her on. I'm suggesting we ask her to dance with us."

Jason sighed heavily, "Fine."

"And we need someone to control the lights for us."

"You've got grand ideas, don't you?"

She smiled at him.

"I'll ask Markus to run the lights. He liked you."

"You're sweet."

"Like sugar?"

She shook her head, "Saccharine."

They both laughed and he playfully shoved her

over, "You're mean."

She sat up and shoved him back. He grabbed her and pulled her on top of him as he fell over.

"Hey, we've got work to do."

"You know what they say about all work and no play."

"It makes you a cliché?"

He feigned being stabbed in the heart, "I live to be cliché."

She gave him quick kiss then climbed off of him, "Time to dance." She patted him on the thigh and climbed into her chair.

He tossed his towel aside.

∞∞∞∞

CHAPTER TWENTY-FIVE:

*L*idia and José sat on their rear deck looking out at the night sky. The stars shined through the pollution from the nearby city as the light to the earth below. José took a sip of his drink as Lidia spoke.

"I've never seen him this dedicated to anything in his life."

José nodded.

"Maybe he's turned a corner," she continued. "Maybe he's finally found what he's been looking for."

"You mean a girl?" asked José playfully.

Lidia smacked his arm then paused in thought.

"Maybe," she said. "But there have been other girls."

"It's different when you find the one though." He smiled at his wife and she felt the love emanating from him.

"Is it?' she teased. "It must be different for girls."

"Ouch." He feigned like he'd been stabbed in the heart.

Lidia looked at him with adoration. How had she been so lucky to get a man like this? She only wished her son would grow to be half the man her husband was.

She wondered what she would ever do without him. If suddenly he were taken from her life. Would she end up like Alex's father, or worse?

She was lost in thought when a shooting star crossed the sky.

"Make a wish," José said.

She snapped out of her trance, "Huh?"

"A shooting star. Make a wish."

"I wish our son would find a relationship as good as ours."

José held up his drink in salute before he took a sip and stared off into the depths of space.

∞∞

CHAPTER TWENTY-SIX:

Markus and Alex sat behind a light board in

the auditorium at the school. The room was dark and only their faces were illuminated by the small desk light clipped to the board. Markus had his fingers on a few of the sliders and he gently pushed one up. As he did so a spot light grew from darkness to a brilliant white. And underneath it stood Joy. Markus hit play on the computer next to him and music surged forth from the speakers. Then Joy began to dance.

Her movements were graceful and primal at the same time. She flowed across the stage. She crouched.

She leapt. Her solo routine mesmerized Alex - until Jason appeared in her light. They danced together flawlessly. They moved as one, limbs entwined, until they broke apart. Their eyes and hands longing for each other as they drifted further apart on stage. The lights followed them then went dark.

Alex was speechless. There was passion in their dance. She saw it. There was a connection between them. She felt it. They belonged together. She knew it. She thought about her future and how she'd never be able to move like that again. She'd never be a partner equal to Jason. And he deserved one. Was she being selfish making him dance with her? But it was his idea. But that was before she got injured. But seeing them together, how could she hold him back? But, but but...

"That was beautiful," she said instead. "Can we do it again?"

The four of them sat sprawled out on the floor with a couple of nearly empty pizza boxes. Sweat drenched their clothing; except for one.

"You guys all look so tired," Markus teased.

Jason threw a piece of crust at him.

"Anybody have plans for Christmas?" Joy asked.

Markus shook his head.

"Same old family stuff," Jason said.

Alex hadn't thought about Christmas. She'd been so wrapped up in this mission that she'd forgotten she was an orphan now. Her demeanor shifted as she thought about her parents. Her face fell and she climbed into her chair, "I'll be right back." She wheeled herself off stage.

After a moment, Joy nudged Jason, and when he looked at her, she nodded towards where Alex had disappeared to. He got to his feet, "Right." And he went off after her. Joy and Markus watched him go then looked at each other and smiled.

Jason found Alex backstage, just sitting silently

in the dark.

"Hey, you okay?" he asked.

She nodded, "Just thinking."

"About?"

"You should do the showcase with Joy, not me."

"Nah, what's the point in that?"

"I'm holding you back. If you dance with her then everyone will see what an amazing talent you are."

"This showcase isn't about me," he replied. "It's never been about me."

"But it should be."

He shook his head.

"I don't want to do it anymore." She couldn't meet his eyes. The lie seared her tongue.

He put his hands on the arms of her chair and bent down to peer into her eyes, but she wouldn't look at him.

"If you aren't going to do it," he said. "Then neither will I."

"You have to."

"I don't have to do anything," he said. "I don't care about this. I don't care about dancing anymore. I'm only doing this for you and if you're done, so am I."

Silence.

She refused to look at him as tears welled in her eyes. She only wanted what was best for him. She couldn't meet his gaze. She knew he'd see straight through her lies. But she couldn't let him sacrifice everything for her. Even if he wanted too. So they sat there in silence. Him staring and her looking away until he gave up and stormed out leaving Alex to sit alone. She cried to herself, silent tears.

After a few moments, Joy emerged from the shadows.

"Jason says we're done?" she accused.

Alex shook her head, "I am, but you two should do it together."

"Why?"

Alex looked at her, "I watched you. You two have a connection. You belong together.

"Jason and I have known each other for over 15 years," she said. "At one time I thought we'd be together, but we won't. What you see as a connection is just history. We know each other."

"That's what I mean. You two really know each other."

"And I know him well enough to know that his heart isn't in ballet. It hasn't been for a while," she said. "That passion you see out there. That's new. That's because of you."

Alex shook her head.

"I would love to have had Jason want me," she continued, "but he doesn't. He wants you. He could have chosen any girl. He picked you."

"You just feel sorry for me." Alex looked at her with tear stained cheeks.

"The only thing I'm going to pity in you is if you're dumb enough to push a great guy away," she said.

"You need to fix this." And Joy walked away.

After a moment, Alex scrubbed at her face to wipe away the tears and wheeled herself back out to the stage. As she arrived, Joy and Markus were making their way out of the theater. Jason sat in a chair, rolling a small piece of pizza over and over in his hand. He looked like he was contemplating the creation of the world and human existence on cooked dough.

Joy waved back at them as she exited, "See you tomorrow." And the door closed leaving Alex and Jason alone.

She rolled up to him, "I'm sorry."

"I know." He looked at her. "I know this is hard and you don't have to do it. Not for me. Not for anybody else. Do this for you or don't do it at all."

"I'm tired of focusing on myself," she replied. "It feels like that's all I've done for years. I don't want this to be for me. I want it to be for us." She put her hand in his. He let the pizza drop to the floor as their eyes met. They stayed that way for a moment, letting their emotions connect with a look in a way that words couldn't communicate.

Okay," he said. "For us."

∞∞∞∞

CHAPTER TWENTY-SEVEN:

Lidia, José, Alex, and Jason decorated a

Christmas tree. Alex rifled through a box packed with newspaper wrapped ornaments. As she unwrapped them and passed them to Lidia, Lidia told her little stories about each one. Alex unwrapped an ornament of an old-fashioned rocket ship and passed it to Lidia.

"I remember this one," Lidia said. "Jason, do you remember?" She showed him the ornament.

He shook his head.

"It was from when you were about 8 years old.

You were obsessed by Ziggy Stardust. You'd run around the house singing Major Tom."

"Four, three, two, one..." José began singing the countdown.

Jason gave his dad the evil eye and Alex chuckled.

"I'm so glad we get to do this," Lidia continued. "I feel like I haven't seen either of you for more than a few minutes since you've been back."

"We've been busy," Jason replied.

"I know. I'm just happy you're here now."

"You've both been working so hard on this showcase," José added.

Alex jumped in, "You're going to come watch, right?"

"We wouldn't miss it."

"We're expecting great things," Lidia said as she draped lights around the tree.

Alex smiled, "It's definitely going to be

something you've never seen before."

"Should I be worried?"

Jason quickly interjected, "Alex put it all together."

"There have been some pretty innovative pieces that have come out of the student showcase over the years. I'm excited to see what you've come up with."

"This is definitely innovative," Alex said with a grin.

José placed the star on the top of the tree, "You're mother's not going to regret bending the rules, is she Jason?"

He shook his head.

Alex replied, "We would never put you at risk like that."

Lidia patted Alex's hand, "He was just being playful, dear." She gave her husband a cautious look. "Have you decided what you're going to do after the showcase?"

Alex shook her head as she wheeled back from the tree to get a good look, "I've been so focused on this and my physical therapy that I haven't given it much thought."

"There are some great universities around here," José added.

Alex nodded, "Once my parent's house sells, I'll look into getting my own place."

"I didn't mean…" José stammered. Lidia put her hand on her husband's shoulder and addressed Alex, "We want you to know you're welcome here for as long as you'd like to stay."

"Thank you, for everything," Alex responded and an awkward silenced ensued until Jason changed the topic.

"I'm looking forward to a break after tomorrow night. Maybe some beach time. What do you think, Alex?"

She smiled at him, grateful for the distraction, "That would be perfect."

Lidia and José exchanged a knowing glance.

"Are you two officially dating?" José taunted.

Alex flushed red and Jason stammered, "C'mon dad..."

"Are you?" Lidia added.

"It's not like it's a secret," Jason said.

"You just never told us is all," replied Lidia.

"Yes," Alex answered, "officially."

"Good," said Lidia. She gave Alex a great hug as José watched and smiled.

∞∞∞∞

CHAPTER TWENTY-EIGHT:

*T*he night at The Miami City Ballet theater was

buzzing. Students rehearsed in hallways, preparing for

their on stage performance. Parents, talent agents, staff

and faculty filled the theater. There was an electricity in

the air that a dancer could either tap into and excel or get

fried by.

Alex and Jason watched from the wings as a

group of dancers performed a number from *Swan Lake*.

The audience sat silently, intensely engaged as the

dancers moved and leaped across the stage. The music

filled the auditorium as the performance continued.

Alex nudged Jason and he leaned down to hear her.

"I'm nervous."

"Everything will be fine," he assured her.

"That's easy for you to say," she smiled. "You've got nothing to lose."

"Is that right?" Jason mocked offense.

"Your parents will love you no matter what," she teased. "Even if they think you're nuts. And you've got to tell them sometime." She shrugged.

"So, why not embarrass them publicly in front of all of their friends and colleagues?" he shrugged back at her and chuckled.

"You're an amazing poet," she assured him. "They won't be embarrassed. You'll see."

"I'm not so sure about that."

Alex grinned, "So you are nervous."

The music stopped and the dancers took their bows to solid applause.

"One more group then we're up," Jason said. He bounced up and down to shake out his limbs and his nerves.

"Do some of that for me too, will you?" Alex said playfully. He smiled at her.

Markus and Joy popped by backstage to join them.

"You ready?" asked Markus as he looked out to the stage where a group of three male dancers were taking their positions.

"Your group was great Joy," Jason said.

"You think so?"

"You're a beautiful dancer," Alex chimed in.

Joy smiled at Alex, "Thanks."

Alex peeked out at the audience, "How do you think they'll react? I mean, it's not exactly ballet."

"It's ballet... ish," Joy responded.

"They're going to love it," said Markus.

"Or hate it," said Jason.

"I've never seen you nervous."

Jason glared at him and bounced some more then rolled his neck to stay loose.

Markus got the hint, "I'm going to head over to my place then."

Jason nodded.

"Thanks," said Alex.

Markus kissed her on the cheek, "Break a leg."

She smacked him in the arm as he left.

The male group on stage finished their piece with a brilliant flourish and the audience applauded enthusiastically when they took their bows. Alex thought about how professional everyone was. The dancers were as good as any in the companies that she'd seen. Every student was performing at such a high level, she wasn't sure their piece could compete. It was so different from what everyone else was doing. Her confidence level dropped with each passing moment until the dancers ran off stage past them and silence filled the air.

The house lights and stage lights all went black. The crowd murmured softly then died down to silence once more. In the audience, Lidia and José sat next to the Director and his wife in the pitch blackness. José squeezed his wife's hand as Jason's voice pierced the darkness.

"Dark hypnotic beats pounding, cardiac rhythm rebating flesh.

Pulse racing, veins throbbing with searing circulation, ice that burns.

Emotions swirling in intoxicating haze.

Agony of existence, consuming sagacity.

Redemption falls and rises anew, a phoenix blaze.

Spontaneous human combustion giving birth to crying surrender.

Nostril flare, inhaling divine breath, the winds of eternity.

The body stirs.

Dancing in a neon afterlife."

A lone violin cried out in the silence as a single spotlight kicked on. Joy stood on point, bathed in its glow, unmoving until Jason joined her. They began to dance together, enraptured in each other's movements. They transitioned from one position to the next with such fluidity that they seemed to melt into one another. Passion and romance as they caressed each other and stared longingly into each other's eyes until Joy leaped out of the light and into the darkness. Jason reached for her, trying to catch her, but she was gone. He looked after her, lost in the shadows.

Across the stage a second spotlight kicked on. The sound of a drum replaced the violin; like the beating of a heart. Alex sat onstage, illuminated in her wheelchair, her back to Jason. He looked up and saw her there. Running to her to attempted to get her attention, but she'd turn away from each attempt until in frustration he grabbed the handles of her chair and shoved her across the stage. She glided. And when she came to a stop she spun and looked at him and he at her; stunned.

The drums were joined by violins and a hip-hop melody erupted from the speakers. The two dancers engaged each other. They spun in synchrony as they drew nearer to one another.

When they got close enough, Jason perched in a handstand on the front of Alex's chair while she spun center stage. They moved back and forth across the stage with breakdance freezes while the chair would glide like a skater on ice. They split apart and pop-locked to the beat, completely in sync.

Jason lifted Alex out of her chair and tossed her into the air. She spun 720 degrees before he caught her again and she pivoted around his torso to his back. Her arms and right leg wrapped around him while her left leg hung unused. He danced for the both of them as her hands moved across his body while he bounded across the floor. He spun as she climbed higher on him so that she could bend over his head and he pulled her down in front of him.

Their bodies pressed together, faces mere millimeters apart as her hands caressed his cheek. She slid down his body until her left foot dragged on stage as he strode towards her chair. He stopped and let her slide back into her seat.

Jason moved to the back of her chair as she settled. She looked for him over her shoulder and he dropped to the floor and slid under her chair, between the wheels, to the front where he emerged in front of Alex to her delight. Then he began to spin her chair until she was spinning rapidly with lights reflecting off of the metal and spokes, sparkling with a mystical glimmer.

Jason pranced off into the darkness, leaving her alone spinning in the light until the chair and Alex toppled over sideways as the music hit its crescendo. She spilled out to the ground. Broken.

Slowly she crawled away from the chair, pulling herself across the stage to the edge where she pushed herself to a full standing position. She winced in pain, but didn't shy away from it. The spot light behind her, on her chair slowly faded to black; leaving her alone. Standing.

The lights went out completely and the audience sat in silence for a moment until applause erupted. The house lights came up and the audience was standing. Lidia wiped away tears as she clapped wildly. The Director leaned close to her and spoke in her ear so she could hear him over the raucous applause. Lidia turned to him and responded. Then they faced the stage where Jason, Alex, and Joy had emerged to take their bow.

After the showcase, the school held a small reception in the main lobby. It was standing room only as proud parents hugged their children when they appeared from backstage and faculty congratulated the dancers on their performances. Lidia and the Director stood off in a corner looking over a list of names while José mingled with parents of other dancers.

Each time a new set of dancers arrived, a small

trickle of applause followed their entry. Joy and Markus found their way to the reception and were met with polite clapping. Joy found her parents and was met with hugs and congratulations. She introduced Markus and the foursome began to chat excitedly. Then Jason emerged, pushing Alex in her wheelchair. As they passed through the crowd, conversations stopped and people stared.

They reached José and he greeted them with a warm embrace. Then the crowd began to applaud. The applause continued and rose in volume. They waved for Joy and Markus to join them and when the four were together the crowd began to hoot and whistle. After what felt like an eternity to Alex, the attention died down and families returned to their own conversations. Joy and Markus faded off into the crowd and Alex, Jason, and José were left to themselves.

"I'm so proud of you both," José exclaimed, as he placed an arm across his son's shoulders. "You did it. I don't know how you pulled that off, but it was amazing."

Lidia broke free from the Director and rushed to their side, hugging Alex first then Jason.

"That was absolutely beautiful." She tried to keep tears out of her eyes and failed. "Moving."

"It was all Alex," Jason said. "She designed the whole piece."

"It was quite a story."

Alex blushed, "You work with what you have, right?"

Lidia nodded.

"Did the Director like it?"

"He was absolutely blown away," Lidia answered. "He said you remind him of your mother. But I think you just may have some of your father in there with that brilliant choreography."

"Thanks." Alex looked at her feet. Conflicting emotions at war within her. She wanted nothing more than to be like her mother, to honor her. But she knew, in so many ways, that she was her father's daughter. That's why his breakdown hurt so much, she was afraid she would end up like him. But, was having such a love that when it vanished you couldn't go on really such a bad thing?

The Director made his way through the crowd until he arrived at their small gathering. He spoke to the dancers. "That was quite a performance from you two tonight."

Jason smiled.

"Thank you," said Alex, as she looked up at the new voice.

The Director looked at her. "I understand that your injury is not permanent?"

"They say I'll never dance again."

"My dear, you just did," he said with great pride. "Auditions for the school are still a months away. There's time."

Alex's heart swelled as he complimented her. He thought she was still able enough to audition. And maybe she was, who knew? "I just wanted to show you what I was capable of."

"Well, you did that. What perhaps you are unaware of is that at this showcase we sometimes find promising students who may not go on to become professional ballet dancers. But they show a certain aptitude for another area of professional dance like artistic design or choreography." He looked at her with tremendous seriousness. "And we sometimes offer those students apprenticeships here in those areas."

"But I'm not a student."

"No, you're not. Yet," he said. "But, we do need a choreography apprentice."

Shock, excitement, awe and fear all played across Alex's face at the same time.

"Are you serious?" she asked through a tightening throat.

He nodded. "I know your father was excellent at it, as I'm sure you will be. If you accept."

"Yes, of course," Alex blurted out. "I... Thank

you." She was stunned at the turn of events. She had wanted nothing more than to be like her mother and here she was being presented with an opportunity to be like... her father. She considered the offer momentarily and, in her heart, she knew what she had to do. "But I don't think I can accept. I don't belong here. Not right now."

The Director was shocked, "After all your work to get in?"

"There are things I have to do first. People who are counting on me." She looked at Jason, "I think I'm going to go run my parents' dance school. Back in Hot Springs."

Jason smiled broadly, crouched down and wrapped his arms around her. He whispered in her ear, "I'm coming with you," he said. "But first, I've got some unfinished business."

"I understand," the Director said. He turned to Jason and slapped him on the shoulder. "And you young man. I knew there was a beautiful dancer in there just waiting to come out." Then he disappeared into the crowd, mingling with other families.

"Waiting to come out," Jason chuckled to himself as he stood and turned to his parents, summoning every bit of courage in him.

José spoke first, "What was that poem you recited in the beginning of the performance?"

"Yeah, who wrote that?" Lidia chimed in.

"I did."

"It was powerful," said José. "Passionate."

Jason nodded.

"So was your dancing tonight," Lidia added. "I've never seen you dance like that."

"I never had a reason to," said Jason. "Though...I don't really want to be a professional dancer."

José smiled, "About time."

"What?"

"It's about time," he repeated. "You stayed in this program so long I was afraid you were going to try to convince yourself that you wanted to be a ballerino."

Lidia smiled too. "We could tell you'd grown out of it."

"Then why'd you make me do it?"

"We never made you," she said. "You never asked to do anything else."

"I was afraid of letting you down."

"The only way you'd let us down is if you never figured out what you really wanted," said José.

"I want to write," Jason blurted out. "Poetry."

José laughed, "You're joking."

Jason shook his head.

"Looks like you'll be living at home for a long time." He wrapped his son in a great hug.

"I don't think so," Jason said. "I might be moving to Hot Springs for a while." He smiled at Alex, "Become a Southern Poet Extraordinaire."

Lidia hugged her son fiercely, "Well, that poem tonight was a good start."

CHAPTER TWENTY-NINE:

*T*he sun radiated from a clear blue, Arkansas sky, casting its light on a group of young girls inside the dance school as Alex counted out steps. Sarah was there, her elation at being back apparent on her face. She watched Alex walk with a slight limp and adjust the brace on her leg. Jason sat near the back with pen in hand writing in a small notebook. He looked up and met Alex's eyes then jotted another verse on his paper. Alex moved to begin the music again.

Sarah looked at their reflection in the mirror and smiled as she and the other girls got back into position for the start of their next dance. Alex met Sarah's gaze and smiled back at her. She knew that this was where she should have been all along.

∞∞∞∞

Made in USA - North Chelmsford, MA
1024143_9781706405719
11.15.2019 1633